A Proper Dragon

A PROPER DRAGON

A Regency Gaslamp Fantasy

E.B. WHEELER

Print ISBN 978-1-7360411-0-9

First printing June 2021

Front cover image by Onesketchman via Fiverr, based on "Lady Maria Conyngham" by Sir Thomas Lawrence

Front cover design by Lauren Makena

Cover copyright Rowan Ridge Press 2021

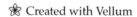 Created with Vellum

*For everyone who knows
that history needs more dragons*

Chapter One

PHOEBE'S MAGIC ALWAYS MISBEHAVED, and if she couldn't tame it, London would be a disaster. The orb of light in her palm bobbed to the tune she hummed. She tried to force it to stay steady despite the jarring pace of her brother's open carriage on the rutted country road. She gently rolled her hand over until the glowing sphere balanced on the back of her knuckles. Then returned it to her palm again. The drizzling January rain hung over the road to London like a gauzy veil, but the light cast a cheerful yellow glow under the folding hood sheltering the bench seat. She allowed herself a smile, but as soon as she stopped humming, the light faded.

She quickly resumed the tune—one of the many dances she had learned for the London Season. Other thoughts crowded the song: presentation at court, fashionable dance steps she couldn't remember, parties with crushes of people. Her heartbeat drummed faster. Exactly when did one curtsey when approaching the queen? What would happen if she didn't get a voucher for the exclusive dancing at Almack's? Her humming faltered.

The light burst apart in a flash like a log spewing embers.

"I say, Phoebs," Max said, glancing up from the reins. "That's a nice trick, but I wish you could do something about this blasted weather."

Phoebe sank back against the cushioned seat and stared at her empty hand. "Yes, perhaps being attuned to wind or water would have been better."

"Didn't mean it like that! Light's a splendid thing too. At least you're attuned to something. No dragon ever came for me."

Phoebe rested a hand on the lump curled up under the rug on her lap—the little green dragon sleeping there, protected from the weather. She smiled at her brother. "You're doing just fine without one. And you're not being banished to London," she added wistfully.

"But I'm happy to stay in town as long as you need me to. Really, I am."

He meant it, Phoebe knew. She longed to be somewhere where she understood what was expected of her—somewhere she wouldn't be lost or in the way—just as much as Max was anxious for the novelty of life away from their country parish. She regarded her brother, perplexed that two children from the same womb could be so different, and he stared back at her, apparently equally as confused. Then they both laughed.

At that moment, there was no mistaking they were brother and sister. Phoebe favored their mother, with her light brown hair and aristocratic Roman nose. Max had darker hair and more of their father's sad hound look about him—until he smiled. Then, everyone said their mischievous grins made them look like twins.

Max turned his attention back to the road. "I'm not needed back at the parish anytime soon, anyway."

Phoebe sighed. That, at least, they had in common.

The wet wind lashed through the open sides of the little gig, and Phoebe wiped her face. The dragon on her lap stirred and uttered a quiet hiss of protest. Phoebe chuckled and scratched under his chin. He rumbled in his throat and settled back to his napping. She stroked the warm, dark green scales of the ridge running between the wings curled closely against his sides, then tucked the rug around him.

Mushroom—the childish name she'd given the hatchling when he chose her as a companion a dozen or so years before— never seemed to take notice when she used her ability. Thus far, the main activities she observed in the young dragon involved sleeping in warm places, eating prodigiously, and knocking fragile items off high shelves in attempts to fly. Yet it was only by being linked to a dragon that anyone could do magic. Perhaps in London, where those with dragons often found their future, she would learn more.

She watched the damp countryside roll by, a familiar monotony of hedgerows and green fields broken occasionally by the movement of sheep. Then a shape by the side of the road caught her eye.

"Stop!" She put a hand on her brother's arm.

"Whoa!" Max drew in the reins. "What?"

"There, in the ditch." Phoebe scooted Mushroom onto the seat and scrambled out of the gig before her brother could stop her. She hurried to the sad bundle of clothes lying beside the road. And within the clothes, a crumpled person.

"Careful!" Max grabbed her arm and held her back. "We should raise the hue and cry. He's probably dead."

"Not he—she," Phoebe said. "And she's not dead. She's breathing."

Phoebe inched forward through the thick, sticky mud to turn over the unconscious figure, ruining the hem of her gown in the process. She was rewarded with a flutter of eyelashes and a confused groan.

"Probably ought not to interfere," Max said. "Might be a thief's trick."

"Nonsense. She's hardly more than a schoolgirl. And look. Her clothes are quite respectable beneath the mud."

Even as she said it, she realized both things made it more likely that the girl was in league with thieves. But her sickly pale skin and uncomprehending stare seemed real enough.

"I think she's had a mishap." Phoebe placed a hand on the girl's forehead. Chilly. "We need to take her somewhere warm and fetch a doctor."

"London's going to eat you alive," Max grumbled.

Phoebe cast him a cutting look to cover her fear that he was right. "We can't leave her like this. Even if she is in league with ruffians, we ought to rescue her."

"Good heavens. Are you going to try to save every urchin in London? No, don't look at me like that! We'll take her to the nearest village, at least."

He helped Phoebe lift the girl, who roused a little and looked around, her eyes wide and uncomprehending. She appeared about sixteen, with the curly blond hair of some ancient Saxon princess. Probably a country squire's daughter.

"We're moving you into the gig, dear," Phoebe said.

They half-dragged, half-pushed the girl onto the seat which was only meant for two. Mushroom, not liking his warm place under the rug disturbed, poked his head out and hissed.

She shrieked and fell back against Phoebe in a semi-swoon. "Oh no! It's one of them."

Max rolled his eyes, and Phoebe tried not to do the same. Her neighbors—far from London where young dragons were a more common sight—had looked askance at her dragon, but none of them were afraid of the creature.

"Shhh." Phoebe held the girl tightly, wondering if she ought to shake some sense into her as her mother would have done.

But it seemed a hard thing when the girl was already weak. "That's just Mushroom. He won't hurt you."

The girl finally managed to focus on Phoebe. "Where am I?" Her eyes widened so much, Phoebe feared a second attack of the vapors. "He's going to find me!"

"Hush, now. The dragon won't hurt you."

The girl's chin quivered. "Not that... *Him*. Please, promise you won't let him get me."

"I promise," Phoebe said.

Max gave her a warning look as he climbed in the other side. Mother would tell her not to be rash, but Father would say they could not turn aside someone in need. Phoebe risked Mushroom's wrath by taking the rug to wrap around the girl's shoulders, hoping the weight of it would force her to still herself. The dragon protested by turning his back on Phoebe and jumping onto Max's shoulder, making her brother grunt at the sudden weight.

Phoebe tried to get comfortable on the crowded seat, though she had to lean out of the protection of the hood a little to fit her shoulders. "Drive on, Max."

As the gig rolled forward again with their new charge squished between them, Phoebe took the girl's icy hand and chafed it. "There now. You see, we're moving. No one's going to catch you."

"He will, though!" The girl burst into tears. "You have no idea! He's too powerful to hide from."

Phoebe and Max exchanged a look asking what they had gotten themselves into, but they could hardly toss the girl back into the ditch now.

The rumble of another set of wheels coming close behind them made Phoebe's chest tighten. Maybe the danger was closer than she had guessed. Max's hands tightened on the reins, but their gig with its single, tired horse couldn't outrun anything more imposing than a farmer's cart. The sound drew closer, and

Phoebe braced herself to see guns draw on her by highwaymen or have a jealous lover overturn their vehicle.

A curricle, lighter than the gig and pulled by a pair of matched greys, swiftly overtook them. Phoebe watched it draw alongside, holding her breath until her lungs ached, but the vehicle showed no interest in running them off the road or waylaying them. The driver, an imposing young man with shockingly pale blond hair and a coldly handsome face, glanced their way and gave a disdainful look at the sight of the little two-person gig with three wet, muddy people crammed into it. Then he rolled past.

She settled back in her seat, her head aching at the sudden burst of relief, and Max's shoulders relaxed. Of course, they wouldn't be alone on the road. All of the *ton* was converging on London for the Season: the lords and gentry for Parliament, their wives for the shops and balls, their sons and daughters for the marriage mart. And Phoebe, among the few who were dragon-linked and attuned to an element and needed a proper introduction to Society.

"There's a village ahead," Max said hopefully. "We could put her up at an inn and call for a doctor, Samaritan-like."

Phoebe wrinkled her nose. It didn't seem the thing to just leave a respectable girl alone at an inn. This wasn't the road to Jericho. She wasn't sure what the responsibility was when rescuing distressed people from ditches, but she had taken it upon herself.

The girl clung to her arm. "Not here. It's too small, and he'll find me for certain."

"What do you propose we do?" Phoebe asked. "Take you on to London?"

"Yes, please!" Her blue eyes lit with excitement. "That's where I was trying to go. Only I grew so hungry and tired. I must have fainted. But if you will take me to London, I could lose myself there."

"No doubt," Max said darkly.

"See, you understand!" The girl said, missing Max's grim undertone. "I could become a school teacher or... or a singer!"

Max made a choking noise, and Phoebe tried not to laugh. Certainly, they were dealing with an innocent.

"It might help us to keep you safe if we knew whom we were hiding you from," Phoebe said.

"Oh, I mustn't! You have no idea... he can be very dangerous. Anyway, it wouldn't do any good. You're not likely to know his name."

Phoebe took a deep breath to keep her voice calm. "Can you tell us your name, then?"

The girl looked down at her lap. "It's Deborah. Deborah, uh... S—Jones."

"Sjones?" Phoebe bit back a grin at the obvious fabrication.

"Sloan," Deborah enunciated. She looked pleased with that. "Yes. I am Miss Sloan."

Phoebe and Max exchanged exasperated looks over Miss "Sloan's" head.

"I'm Phoebe Hart, and this is my brother Maxwell."

Deborah nodded politely to each of them, then seemed to want to press herself back into the seat to disappear. They drove past the small village, and the girl, safe between them, relaxed and fell asleep against Phoebe's arm.

"We're helping a schoolgirl run away from her guardian," Max said quietly. "You realize that, don't you?"

"I see the possibility. But she was sincerely frightened of whomever this person is."

"Might be some sort of depraved murderer. Might murder us for helping her."

He kept his face straight, and Phoebe couldn't tell if he was teasing. "Have you been reading Miss Radcliffe's novels? This is England. People are not kept in towers by villainous counts. Well, not much. But someone might be persecuting her."

"Could just leave her hidden somewhere safe." Max glanced hopefully at the hedgerow along the road.

Phoebe snorted. "We will not!"

"No, I suppose it wouldn't do." Max looked crestfallen.

"We'll just have to take her to Aunt Seraphina's."

Max gaped at her. "Be serious!"

"Well, where else would we take her? Are we going to drop her off at the theater so she can begin her singing career?"

"She is pretty."

"And educated and well-mannered enough that we know she was decently raised. She can't even make up a believable alias. You know what would happen to her on the streets of London."

"Suppose you're right."

"Aunt Seraphina will know what to do. Or, the Bow Street Runners return missing persons to their guardians, do they not? In addition to capturing thieves and rioters?"

"I imagine. But if the guardian is a villain?"

"Well…" Phoebe glanced at the sleeping girl, who looked much younger as she dozed.

"You can't keep her Phoebs, so don't think it! She's not a… a stray dog. Or even a dragon. For all we know, we just helped kidnap her."

Phoebe laughed. "I never thought this journey to London would be the start of my criminal career."

"It's well enough for you to laugh. *You're* not likely to be seen as the mastermind."

"Which is deeply unfair," she said.

"It is! Because the ideas are always yours—even the bad ones!"

Chapter Two

BY THE TIME they reached a larger town, Phoebe's fingers had grown stiff with chill, and she longed to stretch her legs, cramped as they were with Deborah squeezed in next to her. Phoebe and Max exchanged weary looks. They weren't going any farther that day. Phoebe was glad, and not just because of the weather. The closer they got to London, the more she felt like a freshly landed trout was writhing in her stomach.

Max directed the horses into the stableyard of one of the inns. Deborah fidgeted and tried to look behind them as if expecting to see her pursuer, but the only person who took any notice of them was the ostler, ready to help Max trade out the hired horse.

Max helped Phoebe and Deborah down from the gig. Mushroom jumped back onto Phoebe's shoulder, and Deborah flinched from his wings. Still, as they entered the inn, Deborah clung to Phoebe like she wanted to hide under her shadow.

In the shelter of the inn's common room, Mushroom hopped down and shook off the rain. Phoebe's dress dripped muddy water into a growing puddle, and Deborah looked... well, as though she had been sleeping in a ditch. Several of the other patrons gave them disparaging looks, and Phoebe tried to pretend not to notice, though an embarrassed flush crept from her face down her throat. This was not a good beginning. At least the other patrons didn't show much interest in Mushroom as he sniffed around.

"We must be very close to London," Phoebe whispered, more to herself than to Deborah. She began to feel that *she* was the freshly landed trout, wanting nothing more than to wiggle her way back into the safety of the water.

Mushroom's head shot up, his attention focused on a quizzing glass with a gold handle dangling from a young gentleman's waistcoat. The light glinted off the glass as it moved. Mushroom watched it like a cat hunting a bird. Phoebe clicked her tongue at him, trying to get his attention, but he stalked forward, his tail low, his wings folded up, and his neck stretched out. He wouldn't be satisfied until he had added the quizzing glass to his hoard.

Phoebe lunged forward and scooped Mushroom up. He kicked and flapped his wings, smacking Phoebe in the face. Deborah shrank back, looking around like she wanted to escape too, and several of the onlookers snickered. With Mushroom blocking her view, Phoebe stumbled for the stairs, restraining the dragon until Max found her on the landing.

"Trouble?" he asked.

"He saw something shiny."

Max laughed.

"It's not funny," Phoebe huffed.

"I'll have dinner sent up to our rooms."

"Probably for the best." Phoebe managed to tuck Mushroom under her arm, and the dragon responded by going completely limp. "I've put myself on display too much today as it is."

"Isn't that the purpose of London? To be put on display?"

"It sounds very vulgar when you say it that way," Phoebe said, a familiar, anxious heaviness settling in her stomach.

"Suppose it is vulgar. I wish you happy, but I rather hate to see you married off to some stuffy gentleman. None of our other siblings are half as enjoyable to have around as you."

Phoebe's cheeks warmed at the compliment. "Give Charlotte some time to grow up—"

Max waved the thought away. "Oh, perhaps, but, confound it, can't you see I'm trying to tell you I'm going to miss you?"

"I will miss you, too," she said, the heavy feeling making her a little ill. She forced a grin. "I will try to marry someone with a country estate close to home so we may still frighten the children with ghost stories at Christmas and see who can catch the most fish in the summer."

Max gave her a sad smile and returned to arrange for their rooms.

He sent Deborah up along with dinner delivered to a private parlor. After they ate, the ladies retreated to their room, and Phoebe helped her guest try on a few gowns to see if one would fit the shorter girl.

"Do you think we'll reach London tomorrow?" Deborah asked.

"I believe so. Do you know anyone in town?"

Deborah looked thoughtful. "I think my mother had a sister there."

A burden slid from Phoebe's shoulders. They would only have to deliver the girl to her aunt, then. "Do you know her name and direction?"

Deborah looked up, pursing her lips at the effort of remembering. "It was definitely… Janet." She paused. "Or Jane. Definitely Janet or Jane."

"Do you know her surname?" Phoebe asked, trying to keep her voice patient.

"No. My mother died when I was young, you see, and my father didn't get on well with her family."

"Ah." Phoebe's hopes for a quick resolution to Deborah's puzzle evaporated. "And is your father alive?"

"No. He died years ago." And Deborah shut her mouth in a way that made it very clear that she wasn't saying more.

Phoebe encouraged Deborah to settle down for bed, but Phoebe's mind was too full for sleep, so she looked out the window toward London. The girl was an orphan, without any close family. She really could have some sort of scoundrel or schemer after her. She did not strike Phoebe as being a great heiress or anything so fanciful, but there were other reasons wicked men might want to sink their claws into young girls. Phoebe was a preacher's daughter, but her father had not sheltered his children from knowledge of the dangers and heartaches in the world. He had also taught them not to turn their backs on someone in need, even if the person was a bit dramatic and had stolen both of the pillows.

The morning dawned clear, and Phoebe rose with renewed optimism. Soon, they would be in London, and her mother's sister, Lady Seraphina Jasper, society lady that she was, could guide her in both her London debut and the problem of Deborah.

While the girl still slept, Phoebe dressed and headed downstairs to see if Max had bespoken their breakfast. She craved the bittersweet warmth of her morning hot chocolate.

She found the common room nearly empty and frowned at herself. Such a country girl. Members of the *ton* kept late hours. She had just convinced herself that it would be more proper to wait for Max in her room when he stumbled downstairs. He did little more than grunt a greeting and stomp off in search of coffee, but his presence meant that Phoebe could order her hot chocolate and sit to enjoy it with a clear conscious.

Mushroom tried to reach her cup, but she pushed him away. "You know it makes you ill."

She poured a bit of cream into a saucer. Mushroom lapped it with occasional covetous glances at her cup. He then hopped onto the chair next to her and watched out the window with interest. He stretched his wings as if considering trying to fly.

"You'll hit the glass," Phoebe said.

Mushroom flared his wings then tucked them in and hunkered down to growl at the window.

"Not a morning person, either, are you?" she teased him with a little poke.

He yawned at her, showing off sharp teeth and a narrow tongue.

"At least you may enjoy London," she said. "Much more to see there, and other dragons."

She shifted to watch out the window along with him. A dark-haired boy about ten or eleven chased a cat in front of the inn. Through the glass, Phoebe could imagine him calling it, trying to coax it to him. But it darted up a tree, and the boy frowned up at it. After a long moment, he jumped for a branch and, catching it with one hand, tried to pull himself up. He kicked his feet uselessly then dropped back down.

"Oh, that's no way to climb a tree!" Phoebe said and hurried out, Mushroom prancing along beside her.

By the time she reached the tree, the boy dangled from the branch with one foot stretched out to balance himself against the trunk, while the cat looked on with indifference.

"Do you need some help?" Phoebe asked.

The boy looked insulted that she asked, but then Mushroom hopped to Phoebe's shoulder and from there to the branch next to the boy. His eyes brightened.

"You have a dragon!" he said. "What are you attuned to? My

father wanted me to have magic, but a dragon never showed up for me. I think it's a bit late now, don't you? I'm almost twelve, you know. But everyone expected me to have a dragon."

Phoebe stared at the boy. He was well-dressed and spoke in a polished accent, but his questions seemed too personal to be polite. Perhaps it was acceptable among the *ton* to ask questions of those who were dragon-linked.

"They expected a dragon to bond with you?" Phoebe asked.

"Dragons seem to like my family. My father is not linked, but my mother is. And my brother. I think Father was very disappointed that I was not, especially after he went out of his way to marry someone with a dragon." He took a deep breath. "What did you say you are attuned to? I think being attuned to fire or ice would be splendid. But maybe electricity would be better. I could smite people!"

"Yes, very exciting," Phoebe said, struggling to keep up with his train of thoughts.

Her father, if anything, had been disappointed when they found her as a young girl playing with a small dragon. She knew her parents had hoped it would bond with someone else, but the first time she made a little sparkle of lights appear while dancing in the garden, there could be no doubt she was chosen. It was like a curse had fallen on her. A society that wished for their children to have a dragon was a much different world from hers.

"If I was attuned to wind," the boy said, "I could shake the tree branches and get the cat down."

"Hmm. True. But you can still catch him without magic. You started up without a plan, but you just need to do it right—find a foothold."

"A foothold?"

"Yes, like that." She pointed to a likely-looking joint in the tree. "See if you can get your foot there, then pull yourself up."

He gawked at her. "Do you climb trees, Miss?"

"I haven't for several years, but I could outclimb my brother when we were younger."

He grinned and managed to get his foot to the joint, leveraging himself up. Mushroom hopped after him but hung back as if sensing this wasn't his hunt. As the boy grabbed the next branch, Phoebe noticed that he was missing one hand at the wrist. The impediment did not slow him down, though; once he'd righted himself, he simply looped the stub of his forearm over the branch and made quick time catching up with the cat. The creature backed away from him and hunkered down as if daring someone to try to remove him from his perch.

"Joshua!" A male voice boomed. "What are you doing up there?"

The boy—Joshua—looked shaken and clung to the tree as decidedly as the cat. Mushroom jumped down to Phoebe's shoulder and hissed at the interloper, who carried a metallic-blue dragon.

It was the young man with the shockingly blond hair who had passed them in his curricle the previous day. He strode toward them, his blue eyes dangerously cold. He wore a riding coat with several short capes over the shoulders—which Max had taught her was very fashionable—and they billowed around him, though he didn't need any tricks of fashion to make his wide shoulders look impressive. In fact, his entire person was so pleasantly sculpted, from his strong jaw to his muscular legs, that he could have been a statue, except for a nose that had been broken once and healed crookedly.

Phoebe wouldn't be taken in by his splendid appearance, though. This was the second time she had found a young person in some type of distress when this man was around. Nervous shivers ran down her back, but she held her chin up so as not to show her alarm.

She stepped between the man and the tree. "He is trying to retrieve his cat."

He turned his blue eyes on her. "It is not his cat, and I'll thank you not to interfere."

"You are his guardian?"

"I am his brother."

Phoebe looked from the man—with his fair skin and almost-white blond hair—to the boy Joshua—with dark hair and deeply tanned skin—and raised an eyebrow. "Really?"

"I am not accustomed to having my word doubted," the blond man said.

"I am not accustomed to staying silent when something seems wrong to me. You do not look related, and the boy is clearly terrified of you."

The man looked for a moment as if she had slapped him, but he quickly regained his composure. Before she could decide if she ought to apologize, Mushroom hopped from her shoulder onto a tree branch, his gaze transfixed by the quizzing glass hanging from a chain around his neck. His dragon leapt up and spread its wings with a threatening growl.

"Dragon!" he said.

His dragon immediately settled onto his shoulder. Mushroom, seeming to feel he had achieved some kind of victory, crept closer.

"Mushroom," Phoebe called.

The man raised an eyebrow, and she realized how silly the name sounded.

Her dragon ignored her, of course, still intent on the man's shiny quizzing glass. Phoebe tried to grab Mushroom, but he jumped higher, next to Joshua. She put her hands on her hips. This did not bode well for London.

The man raised his quizzing glass and studied Phoebe with well-bred disdain. She felt the full force of that condescending appraisal but glared back at him. Only then did she notice that he wore not one but two black crepe mourning bands on his sleeve. As overbearing as he acted, he could not be older than his mid-twenties. Young to have lost so much. Her anger softened a little with sympathy.

"Please, miss," Joshua said. "He *is* my brother. My half-brother, anyway. Don't smite him, if you please."

The blond man lowered his quizzing glass, looking a little taken aback by this plea, and Phoebe bit her lip to keep from laughing.

"Very well," she said. "I will not smite him as long as he treats you well."

"Oh, West would never hit me, miss. Only, he won't let me keep the cat."

West? Phoebe gave the man a speculative look. The odd things some people named their children. Then again, the man called his dragon "Dragon," so perhaps imagination did not run in his family.

"It has already clawed you twice," West said. "I think it's very clear that it values its freedom."

"But it will starve," Joshua begged.

They all looked at the cat and the branch bending slightly under its considerable size.

"That fellow obviously plays an important role in keeping the local rat population down," West said. "You will leave him here and come down before you hurt yourself."

Joshua hunched his shoulders and, with one last longing look at the cat, began searching for a way down.

"Reach out your foot a little farther for the next toehold," Phoebe called. "There, you have it!"

"Madam," West said coldly. "I believe I asked you not to encourage my brother in his ridiculous ideas of adventure."

"You did say you wished him to come down," Phoebe snapped back.

Before West could respond, Joshua dropped to the ground between them.

West pulled him away, as if trying to protect him from Phoebe. "Are you hurt?"

"No," Joshua said sulkily.

"A little tree climbing is good for boys," Phoebe said.

West gave her a dark look then glanced up at her disobedient dragon, who was still watching his quizzing glass swaying to and fro on its chain. "You may keep your advice to yourself until you have your own house in order."

Phoebe narrowed her eyes. Her dragon might be head-strong, but so was West, and she knew a boy suffering under a too-strict guardian when she saw one.

"Phoebe!" Max's voice came from the inn doorway behind them. "What are you doing out here?"

She relaxed, trying to regain her composure. "I was just helping this young man out of the tree."

Max overlooked Joshua, who was sheltered behind his brother, and glanced instead at West. "What possessed you to climb a tree?"

"We've wandered into a madhouse," West said dismissively. "Come, Joshua."

He dragged his brother off. The boy cast a sorrowful glance at the cat and then waved a quick farewell to Phoebe.

"Isn't the thing to be arguing with men in the street, Phoebs," Max said. "Though I daresay you were right to keep him from climbing the tree. Did he want the cat?"

Phoebe chuckled, too amused to try to clear up the misunderstanding. "I think a cat would do him some good, but this one will be spared that ordeal."

"Probably could have given it a good home. He was wearing Weston, or maybe Stultz."

"Wearing?" Phoebe asked.

"His coat. Very fine. Very expensive."

Phoebe groaned. "So he's probably someone very important,

and I've just made him my enemy. I'm not cut out for this, am I?"

"I don't know. Seemed like you preferred country life. I don't understand why you agreed to come when Aunt Seraphina invited you."

"As much as I like the country, it doesn't like me. The only dragon-linked for miles around? You've seen how people stare at me."

"Hmm. Perhaps London is a better fit. Too bad it wasn't Kitty with the dragon. She would love London."

Phoebe scratched Mushroom's head. As much as she would rather see one of her other sisters in London, she wouldn't let any of them have Mushroom. "Kitty will have her chance. I just have to marry respectably, and then I can bring out Kitty and anyone else in the family who would like the opportunity. I've done enough to ruin their chances at home."

Max looked startled at that. "You? How could you ruin their chances?"

"No one at home knows what to do with me. And... do you remember George Blake?"

"Arrogant runt. Course I remember him."

"I heard him tell Kitty he would have an interest in her if it weren't for her freakish sister. Said he was afraid it might run in the family. A man with a dragon, that's one thing. But a woman? 'What's the use,' he asked?"

"Sounds like you saved Kitty from a miserable end! Or rather, you saved George Blake. If he even looks at any of my sisters, I'll dunk him in the river."

Phoebe managed a little laugh. "Perhaps. But a more... worthy gentleman might feel the same."

"No, he wouldn't! Ridiculous nonsense. Tell you what, Phoebs: you have to stop worrying about what everyone else says. Having a dragon is perfectly respectable. Opens doors for you, even."

"For a man, certainly, but for a woman, the only door it opens is to an alliance with a noble family who wants it in the bloodline. Have you ever heard of a country squire seeking a wife with a dragon? They worry she would appear higher than him. So you see, it's up to me to smooth things over for our sisters, since I've thrown such an obstacle in their way."

"Good heavens! I'm glad I ain't a female. Requires too much thinking."

"Are you making fun of me?"

"Not at all. I always say you're the one with the ideas."

"Bad ideas, you said. Oh, Max, what if this is one of them?"

He shrugged. "Not too late to turn around. Take that girl back to Mother, ask her what to do about it."

Phoebe seriously considered it for a moment, but when she thought of home, she could only imagine her sisters sullenly watching her scare away their suitors. They would marry eventually despite her, but she would remain an awkward burden on her family. That she could not bear. Max had once offered her a place in his household when he came into his comfortable inheritance from their great-uncle, but his eventual wife would not like that scheme.

"No," she said, screwing up her courage. "There's nothing else for it. I must go to London and find someone who will take me, dragon, bad ideas, and all."

Chapter Three

LORD WESTING ESCAPED the little town with all appropriate speed. Less than a year since their father died and left him as the head of the family, and Westing had almost lost his young brother. He heard the echoes of his father's remonstrances. *Careless. Useless. Disgrace.* This was why his father had appointed Uncle Horace and not Westing as his brother's official guardian.

One of his horses tossed its head. He eased up on the reins, which he had been clenching, and glanced over to reassure himself that Joshua was seated beside him in the curricle.

And there had been that woman who thought she knew better than him how to handle Joshua. Who thought Joshua was afraid of him.

"You should not have wandered off," he scolded his young charge.

Joshua dropped the leather strap he'd been using to play with Dragon. "I'm sorry, sir."

"If you do that in London, I shall have you barricaded in your room."

"You wouldn't!" Joshua's attention was now fully on his half-brother.

"Don't test me."

Westing absolutely would do anything to keep his brother safe—and to keep Uncle Horace from taking charge of the boy. Horrible Horace didn't want the bother, but he had very particular ideas about what they owed the family name and would crush Joshua if he felt it would keep the younger generation on his idea of the straight and narrow. Westing remembered it every time he looked in a mirror: Horace had broken Westing's nose as a lesson to obey without question and refused to have it set so Westing wouldn't forget.

"I won't go anywhere without you," Joshua said sulkily. "But please, sir, I want to go out and see things. Fireworks. And maybe some wild animals."

"If you behave," Westing said.

Westing had no interest in fireworks or wild animals. This was his first Season in the House of Lords, and his duties kept him fully occupied. He had to focus on upholding his father's legacy and then returning to oversee the family estate on the coast in Dorset. But his stepmother had begged him to take his brother to London. To broaden his education, she said. Westing wondered if she needed a break from Joshua's rather exuberant exploits. Even a less doting mother might need some time to refresh her energy, and the current Dowager Viscountess was very doting.

"Are you going to let me drive? This is a nice, dull stretch of road for it." Joshua asked, taking up the leather strap again for Dragon.

"Certainly not! I don't wish to end with my neck broken."

"I would not break your neck. Or anything else, either, before you say it. How am I ever going to learn to drive if you won't teach me?"

Westing glanced uneasily at his younger brother. Despite

how Joshua puffed himself up, he still looked so young. Their father had spoken of Eton before his death, but Westing put off the idea. Westing needed Joshua where he could watch him. Keep him safe. And the other boys at Eton might be especially cruel to a lad missing one hand. Perhaps Westing could find a new tutor for his brother in London. That should satisfy Uncle Horace.

"Do you think I'll see that lady in London?" Joshua asked. "I liked her very much. She was more friendly than the rattlepates who usually visit Westing Hall."

Westing snapped a curious look at his younger brother. He could think of plenty of "rattlepates" who had begun dangling after him now that he was Lord Westing, but he didn't think any of them had yet despaired enough to flirt with his eleven-year-old next-in-line. "Which lady?"

"You know, the *dragon* lady. She never did tell me what she's attuned to. She's very mysterious."

"You likely didn't give her a chance to tell you what she was attuned to. And unless she's made her debut, it's not polite to ask."

"*Has* she made her debut, West? You must know who she is."

"I don't think I've ever seen her before, and it's unlikely we'll hear much of her again."

"Don't say that! I bet she takes the *ton* by storm."

Westing laughed. "Where did you learn to talk like that?"

"Mama, of course. She says it about Alexandra, too."

"Alexandra is eight. She has several years before she sets the *ton* on its ears."

"Well," Joshua shrugged off their younger sister with boyish indifference. "If you don't know the dragon lady, then I bet she's coming to London for her debut, and we will see her again."

"She's probably one of several provincial 'dragon ladies' coming to make a lukewarm debut and contract a lukewarm match. She'll raise her inconsequential family a little, and some declining noble household will add a dragon-linked to their ranks."

Joshua sat back and crossed his arms, pouting. "Lady Sophie was right."

"And what did Lady Sophie say?" Westing asked with a laugh in his voice. Their elderly neighbor had no shortage of sharp remarks about everyone.

"She says you're too high in the instep!" Joshua burst out, looking both proud and embarrassed of his boldness.

West laughed. "She's one to talk! But so what if she's right? I have more to be concerned about than the opinion of Lady Sophie. Or of some vulgar, provincial girl."

"She was not vulgar. She just wasn't conceited. And she was very pretty."

"Plain. Brown hair. Brown eyes. Not at all fashionable."

"Her hair was beautiful. It had bits of gold in it. Like honey! And her eyes sparkled when she talked."

Westing repressed a smile. Honey? Leave it to a schoolboy to confuse infatuation with hunger. "She talked too much. Outspoken."

"She was brave. She wasn't afraid of you!"

"She was rude."

"She was kind. She would have let me have a cat."

"That shows her to be lacking in sense."

"No, she was very clever. She knew how to climb a tree!"

"I have no rebuttable to that argument. But the lady is a trifle too old for you."

Joshua flushed. "I'm not going to *marry* her. But I want to be her friend. I bet she marries someone important. A duke or an earl."

Westing doubted this but said, "I wish her well in her endeavors, then."

Dragon leapt up, his long neck stretched to scan the sky, his tongue flicking out in agitation. Westing slowed the carriage. A flapping noise drew his attention to the cloudy sky. A small, pale-yellow dragon glided past them. It looked almost too young to fly, and there was no one in sight.

"What the devil?" Westing pulled the horses to a stop.

The young dragon circled them like a falcon. Westing's dragon flared out its wings. Was this some highwayman's trick? Westing considered reaching for his pistol, but it would only irritate a dragon.

"Who does that dragon belong to?" Joshua asked.

"I don't know, but the person must be nearby."

"Could it be here for me?"

His hopeful tone tore at Westing's chest. Why had their father put such emphasis on Joshua being dragon-linked? No one could control it, and the boy had come to see it as a necessity. A necessity he would never have.

"Dragons only bond with a person when they are hatchlings," Westing said. "This one is too old."

"What if its person is dead?"

Westing nodded. Baron Ross had recently died—been killed by anti-magic Luddites, according to rumor—but his dragon had been red, not yellow. "That could be why it's flying about, but dragons only bond once. If its human died, it will find a flight of dragons in Wales or Scotland until it is old enough to... er, find a mate and then hibernate."

"Oh." Joshua crumpled back in his seat.

Westing frowned and signaled his horses forward. The dragon kept time with them. Odd. What was its interest? Dragon remained on guard, rumbling in his throat and watching the interloper.

The young dragon's pace lagged as it tired, and it drifted down to land on the hood of the curricle. Dragon flapped his wings, hissing at the strange dragon. It bared its teeth, and Dragon lunged at it, spitting shards of ice. The strange dragon growled and looped around, jaws wide, flying directly toward Joshua.

Dragon leapt onto the smaller creature, biting one of its wings. Ice spread from his mouth. The other dragon screeched and tumbled to the ground. Dragon glided back into the curricle, landing to hunch protectively on Joshua's lap.

"What happened?" Joshua asked, his eyes wide.

Westing looked back. The smaller dragon was earth-bound for the moment, running in circles through the grass. "It will be fine when its wing thaws, but I don't think it will pester us again."

"Why did it attack us?"

"I'm not sure."

He'd never heard of a dragon attacking unprovoked. He wasn't sure the dragon meant them harm, but its behavior was very strange. Still, there was much that they didn't know about the creatures.

The sky threatened a storm, but they reached his townhouse in Berkeley Square before the weather broke.

Of course, worse things than rain waited for him in London. While Joshua got settled in, Westing's butler filled him in on the state of the house and presented him with a stack of invitations. He groaned and took them to his father's study.

No, *his* study.

He stood in the doorway for a long moment, half expecting his father to bark at him to stop dawdling. Failing that, it should have been his older brother Herbert there. His father always knew the proper thing to do, and Herbert had been groomed to follow in his footsteps. The only thing Livermore Langley—now Lord Westing—had ever done to please his father was to be dragon-linked. He'd been destined for the army or the navy: somewhere fitting for a hard-headed, lackluster second son. Out of his father's way. Now, however, he had to be the one with all the answers. He was going to prove that his father had been wrong about him. He would not forget what was due his family name.

Dragon hopped down from Westing's shoulder and scuttled into the room to explore. He immediately snatched an empty glass inkwell from the desk and curled up with it behind one of the sofa pillows. Westing chuckled and went to the desk. Other than the missing inkwell, everything was exactly as his father had left it. The paper and pens were in an odd drawer—his father had been left-handed—and it was awkward to reach the family seal, but Westing didn't rearrange anything. Every time he saw the seal, he thought of the family motto: Duty first.

He wrote a note to his man of business about finding a suitable tutor for Joshua. Then he leafed through the invitations. Musicales, balls, card parties. They had been tolerable when he had just been Mr. Langley, able to come and go as he pleased, visit with friends from Oxford, and retire to the country when he grew bored, but now, everything he did had to be correct. He would select only those events he had to attend for propriety.

A invitation in curling black handwriting made him scowl. The Earl of Blackerby. Westing would fob off the meddlesome Secretary of the Home Office as long as possible. The man oversaw state security, an issue which Westing considered none of his affair. His father had often grumbled about Lord Blackerby's schemes, and Westing had no interest in being dragged into them.

Another invitation caught his eye. Lord Jasper. His frown deepened. Lord Jasper was less offensive, but still a menace. As an undersecretary in the Alien Office, he could make trouble for Joshua's mother. That call, at least, Westing would have to return.

Westing was so occupied in sorting his responsibilities, he had almost forgotten about Joshua. His brother appeared in the doorway looking small and a bit lost. Nervous.

He's not afraid of me, Westing reassured himself.

"Joshua," he called.

Joshua jumped, his expression guilty. Westing winced inwardly at that.

"I've settled into my chamber, West, sir," Joshua said. "May I go out into the gardens?"

Westing set the invitations aside and studied his brother's face. "You may. I have work to do, but sometime soon I'll take you to Hyde Park. If you behave until then, I'll let you try the reins."

Joshua beamed and skipped across the room to embrace him. Startled, Westing almost pulled away, but he gave his brother an awkward squeeze. Dragon, awakened by their voices, frisked about the room, and Joshua pulled out a shilling to roll on the floor for the creature to fetch.

Ha! Westing thought, smiling at their antics. Let the honey-haired dragon lady try to tell him how to raise his brother.

Chapter Four

PHOEBE SAT in the middle of the gig's bench for the last stage of their journey. Deborah pressed against her as if afraid of tumbling out. Mushroom sat on Max's shoulder, occasionally batting his hat askew. The rain had stopped, but the sky remained a heavy gray as Max drove to London. Their hired horse trotted along sluggishly, oblivious to the weather.

"Was that thunder?" Deborah asked, practically burrowing into Phoebe's side.

"It might have been." Phoebe tilted her head to look at the steely overcast.

"How I hate storms," Deborah said, her voice barely more than a breath. "Bad things happen in storms."

"I'm sure Max will keep us safe."

Max's lips twitched with a suppressed grin.

They smelled London before they saw it. The wind brought the reek of smoke and animals and river. The horse's pace slowed as the streets clogged with carts and carriages. Phoebe resisted the urge to cover her ears at the din of rumbling wheels, neighing horses, and shouting street vendors roaring around them like a waterfall. How did anyone in London ever sleep with such racket?

Mushroom grumbled at the commotion and hopped to Phoebe's shoulder. Deborah flinched from the dragon and avoided looking at it. In Phoebe's experience, it was more common for people to stare. She had never heard of a dragon hurting anyone unless its bonded person was in danger, but she knew little about dragons. Maybe Deborah had been bitten.

Deborah kept her face turned away from anyone who might happen to glance up and wonder at seeing three people crammed into a gig meant for two. When they passed Hyde Park and entered the fashionable Mayfair district, the girl fidgeted more.

"Your aunt is… is someone important?" she asked.

Phoebe sympathized with Deborah's nervousness. She wasn't sure she was up to snuff with Aunt Seraphina's circle, either. She smiled reassuringly. "She is very kind. Her husband is Lord Jasper, and they move in respectable circles, but you will not find her too lofty."

"That's good." Deborah wrung her fingers and stared down at her lap. "But, because you are dragon-linked, you will be expected to mingle, won't you?"

"Yes, I suppose I will be." Phoebe couldn't decide if Deborah looked wistful or frightened. "Are you wishful to attend a party?"

"Oh, I am!" her eyes sparkled, but then she shook her head. "But, no, I don't want to be seen."

Phoebe patted her hand. Here the girl was, thrust into London's social scene—one she had probably dreamed of—but she was not to partake of it. Not until they could assure her she was safe, at least.

"Perhaps we could attend a masque," Phoebe suggested.

Deb's eyes lit. "Oh! That would be… No, too dangerous. But, oh, maybe…"

Phoebe smiled and didn't push the girl. Finding Deborah's mysterious aunt would be a task to challenge Phoebe's imagination and Aunt Seraphina's connections.

Max delivered them to the front door, where a formidable butler admitted them and bade them wait in the gold parlor. Deborah made a visible effort not to gape at everything from the butler to the gold-colored curtains.

Phoebe was a bit overwhelmed, too. This butler, Phoebe was certain, would look down his nose at her manservants, respectable as they were. Her father was well off for a pastor, and they moved in the best circles of their country neighborhood, but Aunt Seraphina had raised her household to the heights of fashion, from the gilded plasterwork on the walls to the matching footmen in the corridor. Phoebe felt a flutter of nervousness and pressed her hands on her stomach. Mushroom jumped down from his perch on her shoulder and sniffed at the gilding on a picture frame that was taller than Phoebe.

"Phoebe!"

Her aunt's voice made her turn. Phoebe was ready to curtsey, but Aunt Seraphina swept down the stairs and took her hands, kissing her cheeks. She was a willowy lady with hair the color of Phoebe's and a face showing only the faintest hint of wrinkles. "Oh! You remind me of your mother when we were young." Her eyes glistened as she looked Phoebe over.

Mushroom leapt to Seraphina's shoulder. Phoebe's aunt and the green dragon examined each other in interest. Then Mushroom butted her chin gently with his head and turned his attention to her dangling pearl earring.

Phoebe clicked her tongue before disaster could ensue. Mushroom gave her a rueful look, but he shook his wings out and flapped down to examine a beam of sunshine gleaming over the rug. She sighed in relief. That could have ended their London adventure before it began.

"What a delightful creature!" Aunt Seraphina said. "I must ask after all of your family, but first, who is your... companion?"

Lord Jasper, Phoebe's uncle, chose that moment to stride into the entrance hall. Aunt Seraphina straightened, her smile turning a little stiff. Lord Jasper surveyed all of them, his gaze coming to rest on Deborah. His grizzled eyebrows lowered, and he raised his quizzing glass. Deborah trembled like a rabbit facing a hound. Phoebe's stomach flip-flopped, but she had made her choice, and now she would face the consequences.

"Aunt Seraphina, Lord Jasper," she said, stepping between her uncle and his quarry. "May I present Deborah Sloan? She was on her way to London and encountered some difficulties, so we brought her the rest of the way."

Deborah curtseyed deeply, her cheeks pale, and for once, she seemed unable to find her tongue.

"Ah, of course," Aunt Seraphina said with a look at Phoebe that clearly said, 'We will speak more of this later.'

Lord Jasper grunted and marched on his way. Aunt Seraphina watched him go, her face lined with sadness.

Then, she put her smile back on. "I will show you ladies to your rooms, and Phoebe, you will tell me all about your brothers and sisters. Maxwell is seeing to his horse, I suppose. Men are always off doing something or another important, aren't they? How is my dear sister?"

Aunt Seraphina took Phoebe's arm, and they caught up on family gossip as they ascended the stairs. Phoebe clicked her tongue for Mushroom, who romped up after her, poking his head through the rails of the banister to survey the domain below. Deborah followed quietly, not obviously listening, though Phoebe was sure the girl was taking everything in.

Her aunt saw Deborah to a guest room and sent the maids away before taking Phoebe to the chamber that would be hers. It was bigger than the room Phoebe shared with Kitty at home. A window with a narrow balcony looked out over the little garden below, a tiny patch of green in the gray of the city. Mushroom jumped from Phoebe's shoulder to the railing of the balcony and peered down.

"Mushroom!" Phoebe warned.

The dragon lashed his tail and scooted away from her, flexing his wings.

Aunt Seraphina watched with her brows drawn together. "Your dragon is called Mushroom?"

"Yes." Phoebe went to her trunk to fetch her little collection of jewelry: some pearls, a garnet brooch, and an opal bracelet, all loaned to her by her mother. She also brought out Mushroom's collection of knick-knacks ranging from a broken string of false diamonds made of paste to a clipped shilling and a broken spectacle lens. "I know it's a silly name, but he's stuck with it now."

"Oh, dear."

"What's wrong?" Phoebe placed the treasures on a cushioned chair, all except the bracelet, and Mushroom scrambled inside to guard the little hoard.

Her aunt grimaced. "It's just that... 'mushroom' is slang. Rather crude. It means a vulgar person who is trying to rise above their place. You know, they spring up suddenly."

Phoebe blanched. "I had no idea." This was not a good start. She stared at her mother's opal, the flecks of colored light inside the white stone glittering in the sunlight. Some people said bits of magic were trapped in opals. Her mother hoped it would bring her good luck.

"You had no way to know." Her aunt smiled weakly. "But, tell me the rest of the story. About that girl."

Phoebe gave her aunt a quick summary of finding Deborah, the girl's fear of some man chasing her, and the mysterious Janet-or-Jane. Seraphina sat listening with a faint frown.

"Did we do right, Aunt Seraphina?"

"Oh, I don't see what else you could have done. We don't

want some rascal to find such an innocent child. We shall try to keep her out of the public eye. If anyone does see her, we'll pass her off as your school companion."

"I did not attend boarding school."

"Well, the girl is too young to be a duenna and too genteel to be a maid." Aunt Seraphina pursed her lips. "We could dress her in veils and say she's a Spanish lady."

"Do they really wear veils?"

"Goodness, I don't know, but I dare say no one else does either, so we could pull it off if we hide that blonde hair. But do you think we can safely leave her here unattended when needed?"

"Do you mean her safety or the household's?"

"We're on Grosvenor Street, dear! She will be perfectly safe. But what your brother said about thieves does trouble me."

"I haven't seen anything about her that suggests that kind of dishonesty. I'm sure Miss Sloan isn't her real name—"

"You think not?" Aunt Seraphina asked, her hand to her chest.

Phoebe was glad Max hadn't made his way up from the stables yet or she would not have been able to keep a straight face at her aunt's incredulity. "She is trying to hide from someone, aunt. But even that lie she told poorly. I don't expect her to admit a band of thieves as soon as you turn your back."

Aunt Seraphina looked thoughtful. "And they would have to get past the first footman. He's a boxing aficionado. Very well, I will trust your estimation of her, dear. Your mother is very clever, too." She smiled fondly and took Phoebe's chin to study her face. "So like her! I look forward to introducing you to society. I'm certain you will take! We are promised to hold a card party in a few nights, and I will make sure you show to your best advantage."

"Is that proper?" Phoebe asked. "Before I've had a formal debut?"

"Oh, it's a private party, so no one will think anything odd about it. And your uncle always has these little gatherings to entertain political friends."

Phoebe shrank from the idea of a party of strangers, but this was why she had come to London. Her parents didn't know what to do with her, so she had to hope there was a place for her here.

Aunt Seraphina turned her attention to Phoebe's trunks, and they aired the clothes Phoebe had carefully packed. Phoebe watched her aunt expectantly. She had brought her best gowns, made over to match the latest fashion, and her mother had even scraped together enough for two new gowns from a notable local seamstress. It was a woman's form of gambling: investing in the best fashion with the hopes of attracting some eligible young man who would raise her beyond her initial outlay.

But Phoebe could tell by the faint disappointment in her aunt's eyes that their bet had not been good enough. Aunt Seraphina lifted first one dress and then another. Her forehead wrinkled when she saw the muddy gown Phoebe had managed to wrap and pack away so it would not dirty any of the others, but she didn't ask any questions. Finally, she lifted a very light yellow gown with pale green sprigging—one of the new ones—and held it up to Phoebe.

"This one is best, I think. We will take you shopping tomorrow, but this gown is simple and becoming, and it matches your dragon; it will do well enough for any gathering before your debut. That will be soon, you know."

"Oh, will it?" Phoebe tried to absorb the idea that her gowns must match her dragon. Pale yellow was acceptable, but she did not look well in green.

"You're nervous, dear? You needn't be. The Queen's Drawing-room for all the new young ladies who are dragon-linked will be held together in just over a week. That will serve as your formal come-out. You won't be put on the spot alone that way, and though some girls do become a tad competitive about it, you'll only be on center stage for a few minutes."

"Competitive? On center stage? What do you mean? I thought I only was to be presented."

"No, dear. Did you not know? Dragon-linked girls who are presented are expected to put forth a demonstration of their abilities for the court."

"In front of everyone?" Phoebe squeaked. "The Queen? The Prince Regent? Everyone?"

"Yes, but it is quite a friendly event. There's even a grand Dragon-linked Ball after. Always the affair of the Season."

Phoebe sat heavily on the edge of her bed and clutched the opal bracelet. How was she supposed to explain that her magic —silly as it was—also didn't work right? Now, everyone in London would know, and she might as well crawl home to live under a cozy rock because she was sure to be the laughingstock of the Season.

Chapter Five

LORD WESTING STOOD in serious peril of losing his valet, Jenkins, all because he wanted to be on time for his appointment with Lord Jasper.

The valet, whose long face drooped further when he was displeased, gave his master a baleful look. "Your boots, sir, are not fit to be seen."

"It can't be helped," Westing told him. He flicked a stray glass button for Dragon, who chased its eccentric path across the floor of the bedchamber. He admired the boots, which Jenkins had polished to a mirrored black. "Besides, they never looked this good in Dorset."

"This," Jenkins said with a sniff, "is not Dorset."

Westing tried to suppress a smile. "Worried what the other valets will think?"

Jenkins didn't respond immediately but then grumbled, "Prichard will say I'm putting the family to shame."

Westing's jaw stiffened at the mention of his father's haughty manservant. "Prichard is no longer the valet to the Viscount Westing. Remember that, Jenkins."

Jenkins straightened his shoulders. "Yes, sir."

"Dragon, come," Westing called.

Dragon hopped onto his shoulder, his tail lashing slowly against Westing's back, a reflection of his master's agitation. They could not afford to keep Lord Jasper waiting.

Westing paused before leaving to adjust the mourning bands on his arm. This would be about his stepmother, of course. The woman had enough to worry about between being a widow in a strange country and her fears that Horace would take Joshua from her. That might be what Lord Jasper wanted to discuss. The law gave few rights to mothers, and fewer still to foreign ones. Jasper could be warning Westing. Or threatening him.

"You're going out already?" Joshua accused him from the stairway. He held a dragon-shaped kite in his hands.

Westing looked away. He owed his brother a drive in Hyde Park, but he wasn't going to worry the boy about the threat that hung over him. "I have a visit I must make."

Joshua looked forlornly at his kite, then his face brightened again. "While you're gone, can I visit the stable and see the horses?"

"Just don't harass the grooms."

"Thank you!"

Joshua bounded off. Westing watched him grimly. Lord Jasper had best not harass any member of his family. He decided to walk the short distance from Berkeley Square to Grosvenor Street, as it would be quicker than trying to take a carriage or chair. Best get this meeting over with.

The butler at Grosvenor Street ushered him in, guiding him to Lord Jasper's library.

Dragon, perched on Westing's back, suddenly perked up, sniffing the air with interest. Westing hesitated. Lord Jasper did not have a dragon, but...

The doorway of the library looked darker than it should have. Like a confusion of shadows stretched across the threshold. He might have imagined it, but Dragon hissed and leapt down from his shoulder. Now he had no doubt.

Lord Blackerby.

Westing looked back toward the front entrance, but there was no dignified way for him to escape now. He had walked into Blackerby's trap. He let out an exasperated sigh, with only the butler as a witness to his annoyance, then put on a blank face and strolled into the room.

Lord Jasper, a lean man going thin in the hair and thick in the eyebrows, stood ramrod straight to greet Westing. But the Earl of Blackerby lounged in a chair. Shadows—shadows that did not belong to him—swirled on the floor beneath him like a black mist. His deep gray dragon stretched out in the shadows as a cat might lie in the sunshine.

Blackerby smiled sardonically when Westing cast him a disapproving glance. "My dear Mr. Langley... No, forgive me, I mean Lord Westing, don't I? So glad you could join us. I hope you were not put to too much inconvenience, calling so soon after arriving in town."

He propped his feet up on the table. Lord Jasper winced but voiced no objection.

"Not at all," Westing said coolly. He cast one slighting glance at Lord Jasper, who had the grace to look chagrined at the trickery, but Westing would not give Blackerby the satisfaction of complaining.

"Excellent." Blackerby twirled his quizzing glass between his fingers. "Down to business, then."

"Well?" Westing asked.

Blackerby and Jasper exchanged a look, and Jasper cleared his throat.

"The nation is in dangerous straits, as you must be aware." Jasper looked more at ease now, on familiar territory. "Napoleon's anti-dragon campaigns threaten us and our allies. The Irish want to be led by their own Catholic dragon-linked.

And the Luddites among us would see any form of magic dispensed with. We—the Home Office and the Alien Office," he gestured between Lord Blackerby and himself, "are watching as much of England as we can, but we need eyes everywhere."

"And if I see anything suspicious, I will, of course, report it," Westing said. "Now, if that is all—"

Blackerby stood. The man was tall, his face angular, and the shadows settled around his feet like a dark gossamer cloak. "None of that, dear Lord Westing. You are in a unique position to help us."

Westing glanced at Dragon, who sat hunched on the floor, his tail a blur of blue whipping back and forth as he watched Blackerby's dragon. "You would like me to give the French frostbite?"

Blackerby laughed. "Wouldn't that be delightful? But, no. You are more than just your magic, Viscount Westing."

Westing crossed his arms. "Then what?"

"Your estate is on the coast. Full of, shall we say, stubborn people with independent ideas?"

"And I do my part to stop free trading when it comes to my attention." Westing didn't let it come to his attention often, though. Smuggling was the lifeblood of most people along the coast, with taxes so high to support the war effort. As long as the smugglers weren't hurting anyone—not wrecking ships or fighting over territory—he let their quiet activities go unnoticed, as his father had before him.

Blackerby waved a dismissive hand. "I hardly care about brandy and laces." He glanced at the foppish bit of lace on his shirt cuff and smirked. "Or, I'm not asking questions about them, at least. But what about spies coming from France? Or anti-dragon publications?"

That gave Westing pause. "Not that I'm aware."

"Precisely. We need you to be aware."

"If I hear—"

"No." Blackerby dropped his mocking tone. "We need you to take an active role in rooting them out. Question servants. Seek informants. You have a responsibility—"

"I have a responsibility to manage my estates fairly and represent my local interests in Parliament. To keep the peace. I will be on guard for smuggled Frenchmen or revolutionary propaganda and turn them over to the Alien Office if I find them. But I will not invade homes or turn neighbors into spies. I'll leave chasing shadows to you," he added with a curl of his lip.

Westing turned his back on them, but Blackerby called, "How are your stepmother and your darling half-siblings? You brought your brother to London with you, did you not?"

Westing slowly turned to face them again. Dragon hopped to his shoulder, his claws cold through Westing's coat. Jasper's eyes were wide, and his mouth moved a little in protest, but Blackerby leveled a challenging stare at Westing.

"My lord," Westing said, his voice steady and sharp. "Understand, I was not raised to politics. I will not smile and play word games like my father or older brother might have. Are you threatening my family?"

Blackerby smiled with one corner of his mouth. "Not I."

"Good, because if you do, I will see you go down encased in ice and strangled by the shadows you draw about you. You do not touch my family."

He stalked toward the door. A footman rushed to open it.

Dragon glided to his shoulder and rumbled a warning.

Westing turned into the corridor and slammed into Joshua's dragon lady.

She gaped at him, her green dragon held tightly in her arms. He stared back, not sure how much she had heard of their raised voices.

"What are you doing here?" he asked, his first, irrational thought that Blackerby or Jasper had sent her to spy on him.

"I live here," she said. "But you needn't snap at me just because my uncle has annoyed you."

He glared at her, in no mood to be lectured about his manners.

"Oh, I wasn't spying at keyholes, if you're thinking anything so poor of me. I only wanted something to read."

With that, she continued on her way. Her dragon looked back at Westing and flicked its tongue out, and he almost laughed at the rude-looking gesture. Dragon grumbled and lashed his tail in return.

He shouldn't have been surprised that the outspoken girl was part of such an insufferable household. He *was* surprised to feel a flash of sympathy toward her, though. At least she seemed honest, which was more than he could say for Jasper or Blackerby.

Blackguards.

If only he knew how his father had dealt with them. The late Lord Westing would never have been bullied into acting as a spy, but if his father had spoken of it to Herbert, the knowledge was now lost along with the boat that took them both to the seafloor. Their father hadn't bothered confiding in his second son.

Regardless, Westing had nothing more to say to Blackerby or Jasper. He brushed past the confused butler and strode back to Berkeley Square and his brother. They had a kite to fly.

Chapter Six

Phoebe wanted something for poor Deborah to read while in hiding, but she wasn't going to stand outside the library and let the shockingly blond man glare at her all afternoon. Why couldn't her uncle have found some other place to argue with his guests? To threaten them, from what Phoebe had accidentally overheard. As rude as the blond man was, Phoebe applauded him for standing up to her uncle. But why would Uncle Jasper threaten anyone?

Mushroom, sensing her unease, rubbed his head along her jaw and gazed at her with shining black eyes. She sighed and scratched under his chin.

Deborah stood when Phoebe returned to the upstairs antechamber they used as a clandestine sitting room. "You look pale. Has anything happened? Is someone searching for me?"

Phoebe set Mushroom down and drew Deborah back to the settee. "No. I came upon a little quarrel taking place downstairs, but it has nothing to do with us. Would you like another game of backgammon?"

While she entertained Deborah, Phoebe tried to convince

herself that her uncle's affairs had nothing to do with her. If Max
were there, he would certainly agree, but her brother had run off
to visit school friends.

When she was alone with her aunt later, she couldn't help
asking.

"What exactly does uncle do? My father is busy all day with
his parish, but I thought gentlemen with titles just went to
Parliament and managed their estates."

"Oh." Aunt Seraphina's brow wrinkled. "I suppose that is
what most of them do."

"But it seems my uncle spends most of his time in London."

"True, dear. He's an undersecretary for the Alien Office. They
make certain no spies come over from France, that sort of thing."

"Oh." The odious blond gentleman didn't sound French, but
spies wouldn't be that obvious. Phoebe fancied the idea of him
being some kind of wicked foreign agent. It would make it
acceptable for her to dislike him, and it wouldn't matter so
much that he despised her. But it was his family he had been
defending. His half-brother didn't look much like him. The boy
could be foreign. But Phoebe bristled at the idea of anyone—
especially her uncle—threatening a child.

"Dangerous people don't come to the house, do they?" she
asked.

"Goodness, no! At least, I shouldn't think so," her aunt said
dismissively. "And the first footman boxes, remember. You're
perfectly safe here."

Phoebe sensed she wasn't supposed to ask about her uncle's
work. It was not her affair. Not proper.

Her aunt's expression brightened. "Tomorrow we see my
dressmaker, Mrs. Reynolds, about your court gown. If you don't
mind, I would also like to visit an old school friend of mine,
Mrs. Jonston." She lowered her voice and leaned forward
confidentially. "Perfectly respectable herself, but she made a
poor choice in husbands, I'm afraid. Charming man, but he was

addicted to gambling and left poor Isabella in a dire position when he died."

"I would be delighted to meet her," Phoebe said. And she would enjoy being fussed over by a fashionable dressmaker. A more proper occupation for a lady than worrying about spies.

"You should also practice your magic for the Queen's Drawing-room."

Phoebe glanced at Mushroom, who scratched his muzzle with a foreclaw and sneezed. No reassurance there that her magic would behave. "Do you know what the other ladies will do when presented?"

"Oh, heavens, no! It must remain secret. If people knew, they would always be trying to show each other up."

"Don't they do that anyway?"

"Well, yes, but they can only guess what the others will do, so it's a little less vicious."

Phoebe groaned, but she at least needed to put on a good face. "Are the other young ladies all... well, are they all good at using their magic? Does anything ever happen with it that they don't intend?"

Aunt Seraphina looked at her in alarm. "I don't know, dear, not being attuned myself. But if so, it's never obvious. Whatever you do, it must *appear* that you are in perfect control."

Phoebe sat back heavily and scratched behind Mushroom's wings. She wondered if it was too late to have Max take her home. But all of her family would be so disappointed.

Aunt Seraphina turned her attention to planning the menu for the card party. Phoebe lifted Mushroom and wandered down the corridor to the ballroom. In one corner stood a pianoforte. Her mother had made certain she could play well; since she had no great skill at drawing, she needed some accomplishment.

Phoebe sat before the rectangular instrument and touched the smooth ivory keys. The familiar scents of wood and lacquer drifted around her. Mushroom curled up next to her on the bench. Phoebe took a deep breath and began a minuet. After several measures, a few weak flickers of light popped up, pulsing in time to the beat, but they vanished almost instantly. Phoebe tried to put more feeling into the music, but no other lights appeared.

Phoebe stopped. The last notes hung in the air longer than her magic had. She stared at where the lights had blinked out of existence, a sick dread growing in her stomach.

"What am I to do?" she asked Mushroom.

The dragon rested his head on her lap and sighed, but he offered no answers.

Chapter Seven

THE FOLLOWING DAY, Aunt Seraphina and Phoebe climbed into the Jaspers' carriage, carrying a basket of food from the kitchen. Aunt Seraphina directed the driver to Fleet Street.

The name of the street famous for its newspapers and printers piqued Phoebe's interest. Some of her favorite books had their birth in Fleet Street. As the Jaspers' carriage bore her and Aunt Seraphina east through the crowded streets, she craned to see more. Mushroom put his foreclaws on her head to get a better view, disarranging the flowers in her bonnet.

As they drew closer, the stink of the river mingled with the scents of ink and roasting meat and coffee. Men in their high-collared shirts and white cravats scrambled in and out of the shops, publisher's offices, taverns, and coffee-houses lining Fleet Street, like ants in a colony.

The driver stopped, and Aunt Seraphina guided Phoebe up to a set of rooms above a coffee-house. Aunt Seraphina knocked, and an elderly housekeeper admitted them to a humble parlor with worn chairs and a sagging sofa.

A lady with auburn hair tucked under her white cap stood

and held out her hands for Aunt Seraphina. "My dear Sera. It is too good of you to visit."

"Belle, you look as lovely as ever." Aunt Seraphina motioned Phoebe forward. "Isabella, may I present my niece, Phoebe Hart, here to make her debut. Phoebe, Mrs. Jonston."

"A pleasure," Mrs. Jonston said with a sincere smile. "Lady Jasper, Miss Hart, I don't know if you're acquainted with my cousin, Lady Amelia Sharp."

A young lady with coppery red hair stood from a chair in the corner. Phoebe gave a start, for she had not realized Mrs. Jonston had a guest. The young woman was about Phoebe's age, with a face that might be said to be more interesting than pretty, and a lively intelligence in her eyes.

Aunt Seraphina smiled. "Lady Amelia has no reason to mingle with old married ladies like myself, but I have seen her dancing very prettily on several occasions."

Lady Amelia inclined her head in acknowledgement.

Aunt Seraphina presented the basket to her friend. "Lord Jasper caught more fish than Cook can use, so I thought you might enjoy them, and there are some extra mincemeat pies from our last dinner party, as well. You would be doing me such a favor to take them so they don't go to waste."

Mrs. Jonston's eyes shone with liquid gratitude for a moment, but she blinked hard and accepted the basket—and the lie about Lord Jasper fishing—with a graceful smile. Phoebe realized that there were no sounds or scents of baking coming from the adjacent kitchen and wondered just how dire Mrs. Jonston's circumstances were.

The two old school friends fell into conversation, and Phoebe and Lady Amelia were left to eye each other like two peacocks displaying their feathers. At least Lady Amelia did not have a dragon, so she was not one of Phoebe's rivals for the Queen's Drawing-room.

"You are just arrived in London." Lady Amelia said quietly enough not to disturb the older ladies in their reminiscing.

"I am," Phoebe admitted. "Is it so obvious?"

"You have not yet learned to look bored."

"Must I? I find it all so overwhelming, I cannot imagine ever being bored."

Lady Amelia smiled with one corner of her mouth. "Honesty. How refreshing. It is overwhelming at first, though, isn't it. You're to be presented with the other dragon-linked ladies."

Lady Amelia spoke as though she were stating facts, not asking questions, but Phoebe answered anyway, especially since this curious lady responded well to honesty.

"Yes, though I wish I didn't have to be. Have you been presented yet?"

"Last year. I did not take—it's the red hair, I believe, which is not at all in fashion—so I'm here for a second Season, and I'm afraid I do find it rather dull. I'm not dragon-linked, so maybe that adds a little more drama to the whole ordeal. Rite of passage, if you will." Lady Amelia studied her, and Phoebe felt as transparent as crystal. "Some of our fellow young ladies are a pack of harpies, but don't let them intimidate you, and you'll do fine."

"Harpies?" Phoebe asked.

Amelia raised an eyebrow. "Don't trust any of us too much, Miss Hart. Remember, we're all competition, and the stakes are rather grim."

She glanced meaningfully around the sad little parlor, and Phoebe saw the shabby furniture and empty kitchen in a new light: the fruits of a match poorly made, the fate of those young ladies who did not win in London's high stakes matrimonial game.

The thought made her stomach knot, and she was glad when Mrs. Jonston invited them to sit and join the conversation. The main topic was the mysterious murder of Baron Ross.

"I've heard the killer only took one thing: an opal button from his waistcoat," Aunt Seraphina said.

Mrs. Johnston shook her head sadly. "What a tragedy, to be killed over something so trivial."

"If it really was the Luddites who killed him, nothing about it is trivial," Lady Amelia said.

Aunt Seraphina shot a nervous look at Mushroom curled up on Phoebe's lap. "There's no reason to believe the Luddites have resorted to murder. This is not France, after all."

Lady Amelia looked like she had more to say, but she let the conversation pass to safer subjects.

When Aunt Seraphina and Phoebe rose to leave, Lady Amelia checked the watch hanging on a chain around her neck and decided to walk down with them. Mushroom's attention fixated on the light flashing off the watch face, and Phoebe kept a tight grasp on her dragon as they descended the stairs.

Aunt Seraphina's carriage, which had been pacing up and down the street to keep the horses warm, pulled to a stop for its mistress.

A smartly-dressed lady with dark hair brought her low phaeton to a halt behind the Jaspers' carriage. She put one hand on the rusty-orange dragon on her lap and raised the other in greeting. Uncertain, Phoebe waved back.

The lady driver gave Phoebe a sneering look and said pointedly, "Amelia, dear, you had been gone so long I almost despaired of you returning. I bought the new Miss Charity book and am longing to read it."

Phoebe lowered her hand, her cheeks hot. Of course, the lady had not been waving to her.

Amelia gave Phoebe a look full of sympathy and said to the lady in the carriage, "You didn't mind the excuse to shop a bit longer, Millicent."

Millicent giggled. "You have found me out. I did not."

Aunt Seraphina, who had already climbed into her carriage, called for Phoebe.

"Goodbye, Lady Amelia." Phoebe glanced at Millicent. Did she ignore the woman? They were not formally acquainted, but she didn't want to cut her or leave things awkward. She settled on a friendly nod.

Millicent rolled her eyes. "Amelia, if you are going to make acquaintances with all the country girls in London, you could at least remind them that they should not assume a familiarity with their betters unless the connection is *desired* and *invited*. If they don't learn some manners, they will not fare well in London."

Phoebe's throat burned like she had swallowed a coal. She was torn between wanting to lecture this haughty lady on her own manners and rushing to hide in the carriage with Aunt Seraphina.

Lady Amelia turned to Phoebe so Millicent could not see her face and mouthed the word, "Harpy." Outloud, she said, "I hope we see each other again, Miss Hart."

That gave Phoebe the closest to a graceful exit she could hope for. Her cheeks still burned when she sat in the carriage, but the dimness gave her some semblance of privacy. London rolled slowly—very slowly—past, the constant rumble of carts like the grinding of a millstone.

"Tired out, dear?" Aunt Seraphina asked.

"Perhaps a little," Phoebe said, glad her aunt had missed the exchange with Millicent. "And I was thinking. Mrs. Jonston seems young to be a widow and so, well…"

"And sunk so low in society?" Aunt Seraphina sighed. "It's shocking what a blow fortune has dealt her. And Mr. Jonston seemed like such a respectable match."

Phoebe shivered and stroked Mushroom. "Can she not go home? If her cousin is a lady…"

"A lady from a family whose fortunes are reduced, and

Isabella's aunt simply married into the Marquess's family, you see. My poor friend's only close family is her sister, who has six children and a barrister husband with an inconsistent income."

"Better to maintain some semblance of pride rather than become an acknowledged burden," Phoebe said quietly. She understood well enough. "But she is young and pretty. She could remarry."

"I wish she might, but she lacks the funds to put herself forward—and would not accept them from me or any other friend. And even if she did, her husband's disgrace clings to her. He died with many creditors unpaid. It would be odd circumstances that would bring her round right again. But who's to say that won't happen?" She patted Phoebe's hand with a fond smile. "Just... make your choices carefully, my dear."

"I have choices?" Phoebe mumbled to the window.

Aunt Seraphina's spirits rose as they approached Bond Street, the residence of her dressmaker, Mrs. Reynolds. Phoebe's heart sank, however, as she watched the parade of people in the latest fashions: the tall feathers on ladies' hats that looked like a balancing act to wear and the men's high, starched collars that prevented them from turning their heads. Phoebe would look like a child wearing a costume in such clothing. And who was to say the men weren't wearing costumes as well, hiding the vices that would leave their wives in ruin?

The groom let them down from the carriage. Aunt Seraphina walked into the shop as comfortably as she might step into her own home.

"We are here for my niece's court dress," she announced.

The effect was like lightning zapping through the store. Mrs. Reynolds herself—a black-haired woman with a full figure— descended on Phoebe like a crow after a shiny bauble, spinning her about, eyeing her critically but not unkindly.

Her gaze lighted on Mushroom and her eyes shone like Christmas morning.

"Lovely, lovely! The dragon's gold highlights complement your hair. We will make the best of both of them. And what does gold signify? What is your attunement?"

"Light," Phoebe said.

Mrs. Reynolds clapped her hands together. "Oh, fabulous! I have such ideas. You have come to the right place. I hear that Mrs. Glass also is dressing a young lady attuned to light, but have no fear, we will outshine her. Pardon the expression."

Phoebe nodded mutely. Another young lady attuned to light? And it was widely regarded as a competition? She stood very still as Mrs. Reynolds took measurements and talked about embroidery and trains, the words a dull buzz in her ears.

Mushroom wandered the shop, and Phoebe was afraid he would steal pearls or glass beads, but instead he went to sniff at a big tom cat who watched the premises with a lordly expression. Maybe he would behave. Maybe her magic would behave. Maybe she wouldn't die of humiliation.

Phoebe had been afraid she would look silly in the dresses she had seen in the street, but she quickly realized she had underestimated the horrors of fashion about to be inflicted upon her.

"Hoops are still required at court," Mrs. Reynolds explained.

"Hoops?" Phoebe asked, eyeing the contraptions that would give her the size and shape of a giant church bell, and probably less grace.

"Terrible, isn't it?" Aunt Seraphina fanned herself and looked askance at the hoops.

"Never fear," Mrs. Reynolds said around the needle held between her teeth. "I do not make the mistake of employing the high waist along with the hoops." She shuddered. "The court style is old-fashioned, but it can still be charming."

As Mrs. Reynolds worked, a pale brown dragon flapped up

and landed on her shoulder, studying Mushroom's activities
with as much interest as Mrs. Reynolds showed to Phoebe. Mrs.
Reynolds caught her curious glance and smiled.

"You're surprised seeing someone dragon-linked working a
shop?"

Phoebe flushed. "I am, I suppose."

"It is unusual, I admit."

"How... I shouldn't ask, I guess."

Mrs. Reynolds laughed. "Too late. You already have. But I'm
not offended. I don't mind talking about it, especially to another
dragon-linked girl. I was not from a noble family, you see. My
family sent me to London, thinking this would be quite the
place for me. I was dazzled by the fashions always changing.
Always a new challenge. I was less dazzled by the men. A lot of
coxcombs and fops and none of them to my taste. So, I did what
makes me happy. I am respectable, and I decide my own
course."

"That's reassuring to hear," Phoebe said. The "Mrs." was a
title of courtesy, then, the product of years of hard work and
propriety rather than marriage. "What are you attuned to?"

Mrs. Reynolds smiled. "Fire."

"Really?" Phoebe's eyes widened. "Do you use it in the
shop?"

She laughed. "Sometimes to heat up the tea."

That gave Phoebe a great deal to think about. Mrs. Reynolds
and her dragon seemed perfectly content in their life. Would
Phoebe be the same if she did not marry?

Back in the carriage, Phoebe cradled Mushroom in her arms
and asked her aunt, "Who is the other young lady attuned to
light?"

Lady Jasper sighed. "Lady Amelia's friend, Lady Millicent
Blanchfield, daughter of the Earl of Greenley. A rather sharp-
tongued young lady, I'm afraid."

Phoebe sank back in the seat, running her fingers along the

ridge of Mushroom's wing. Of course, Millicent—*Lady* Millicent —would be her competition. Another powerful enemy. Phoebe had a knack for collecting those. She might as well leave now, before all of London was laughing at her.

But her Mama had invested so much in this wasted trip to London, and Aunt Seraphina had just spent a fortune at Mrs. Reynolds' shop. Her sisters prospered with her away from home. She couldn't leave yet. Truthfully, she did not want to crawl home in defeat. If she did return, she wanted it to be because she chose to do so, not because she was chased away.

When they returned to Grosvenor Street, Phoebe found her way again to the pianoforte. She set Mushroom beside her and placed her fingers on the keys, letting her mind roam. Lady Millicent. The Queen's Drawing-room. The aggravating man with the white-blond hair. It all swirled and pulsed and poured out in her song.

It was the same minuet as before but played with a timing and fervor that might have killed anyone trying to dance to it.

A glowing stag sprung to life over the instrument. He bounded around the ballroom, leaving ripples of light in the air where his feet had touched. Phoebe's eyes widened, but she kept playing. When she reached the last notes, she kept her fingers pressed on the keys. The stag vanished in a puff like scattered dandelion seeds. Phoebe's breath came fast.

"Did you see that, Mushroom?" she asked.

Mushroom stretched and yawned.

Phoebe couldn't hope to do anything so impressive for the Queen's Drawing-room, but perhaps she *could* come up with a suitable performance. She just had to avoid embarrassing herself further. If she could get through her aunt's card party, perhaps she could fake the rest of it as well.

Chapter Eight

WESTING SAT at the breakfast table surrounded by *The Times, The Morning Post,* and *The Morning Chronicle.* He skipped the gossip and society pages, skimmed through the crime reports—the Bow Street Runners still sought clues about the murder of Baron Ross—and settled into the political news, weighing each perspective with a view to his role in Parliament. His father had emphasized that his duty in the House of Lords was a sacred trust. He had never warned his younger sons that it was more dreary and thankless than sorting the grains of sand on the beach. While the tide was coming in.

Westing set down the paper and gave a start to see Joshua sitting at his elbow. At home, the boy jabbered on at the breakfast table while shoving toast or ham in his mouth. Now, Joshua sat perfectly straight and quietly cut his cold capon into respectable bites. His expression was a little too innocent.

"Joshua."

The boy jumped and dropped his fork. It pinged off the table and onto the floor. He looked stricken.

"I'm sorry, West, sir!"

Westing realized he was scowling and tried to relax his expression. "Don't give it another thought."

"But Mother said that what you are doing is very important," he said earnestly. Then he dropped his gaze to the smear on the table where his fork had landed. "And I must not be in the way."

Westing took a steadying breath and reached for *The Morning Post*, but Dragon had pulled it to the floor and was shredding it with gusto. He looked at his brother. "You have been a model of good behavior. In fact, I have been able to get so much done this morning that—if the day stays fine—we shall finally go for our ride in Hyde Park this afternoon."

"Oh, thank you! That is, thank you, sir."

Joshua's eyes shone with such excitement that Westing felt a pang of guilt. Was he neglecting the boy? It had to be lonely without his mother or sister or any of the local boys to play with. Westing's man of business was sending over an applicant for Joshua's tutor. At least studying would keep the lad occupied.

The applicant was Mr. Sudbury, a gentlemanly scholar of middling years whose references showed he had been a schoolmaster and then a tutor to several respectable families in the north. Westing interviewed him in the study early that afternoon.

"What brings you to London?" Westing asked.

Sudbury adjusted his spectacles. "It will seem childish to you, sir, but I have a great interest in dragons. I hope that by finding a position in London, I might also pursue my studies."

Westing glanced at Dragon, who watched Sudbury with calm interest. "London sounds like the place for you. I must warn you that I don't make the town my permanent home, but if I find your instruction of my brother satisfactory, I will offer you a good reference when I leave after the Season."

"Thank you, my lord. I believe our needs will suit well if you find everything in my background in order."

Westing hesitated, wishing there was a bit more warmth in Sudbury's expression. He fidgeted with the family seal on the desk. "I would like to be clear on one thing."

"Yes, my lord?"

"My brother has a mild impediment. He is missing one hand."

"Is it his writing hand?" Sudbury asked, showing no shock or distaste.

"It is not."

"Then I do not see that it will be a problem."

"Very good," Westing said, relieved to have found someone to keep Joshua's mind occupied. "You may start on Monday."

Once Mr. Sudbury was dismissed, Westing looked through the rest of his mail. Uncle Horace wrote to ask after Joshua. Westing rubbed his crooked nose and wrote a brief note informing his uncle that he had employed a tutor for the lad. Nothing for Horace to trouble himself over. He was able to call for his horses with the knowledge that he was doing all that was proper.

"Joshua!" Westing called. "I hope you're ready."

Dragon hopped on his shoulder, and Joshua, who had been kicking his heels in the drawing-room, hurried out, nearly bouncing in his excitement to learn how to drive.

Drive was a loose term. Any afternoon during the Season, Hyde Park was thronged with people, and that day seemed especially bad. The great parade of people walking, riding, or driving was so packed that Westing's curricle barely crawled through the park. Westing could give Joshua a couple of pointers in driving without worrying that the horses would run away with them; they weren't running anywhere. No chance of any harm coming to the boy under Westing's care. Not this time.

Joshua adapted well to having only one hand to use on the

reins, supplementing his control with the stub of his other arm. Westing nodded his approval, and Joshua swelled like he might pop with pride.

"Yoo-hoo! Lord Westing!"

Westing closed his eyes in a silent prayer for patience, then turned to see Lady Millicent Blanchfield hailing him.

"Oh, not her!" Joshua groaned.

"Be polite," Westing reminded him quietly.

Dragon hissed, his breath leaving a frosting of ice on the rim of Westing's hat, then jumped down to plant himself on Joshua's lap like a watchful gargoyle.

Lady Millicent was a vivacious, dark-haired beauty, though with a calculating glimmer in her eyes. A rusty-orange dragon lounged on her lap, wearing a diamond collar like a spoiled little pug, and a red-headed lady sat beside her in her low phaeton. Lady Amelia Sharp. Westing wasn't sure what to make of that lady.

Lady Millicent had quite nearly been promised to Westing's elder brother, but she had put off all signs of mourning in time for the Season. She would not let a little thing like death ruin her chances for a good match. Westing was grateful he was under no Biblical injunction to take his brother's almost-widow to wife, though he wondered with a sinking sense of dread if it might be expected of him.

"Westing, darling, I'm so thrilled to see you," Lady Millicent said, ignoring Joshua and Dragon completely. "Have you come to see the dragon, too?"

"The dragon?" Westing glanced at her dragon, but he wondered if one of the older, larger beasts had been spotted. It was extremely rare, as adult dragons tended to hibernate most of the time, but they occasionally moved across the country.

"The rogue dragon," Lady Millicent said, looking gratified to provide some fresh gossip.

"A rogue?" Westing asked, picturing a monstrous creature ravaging the countryside.

Lady Millicent looked at Lady Amelia, who said in her low tones, "A young dragon, unattached, flying about London."

Lady Millicent nodded excitedly. "Yes, they say it's... Oh, what do they say, Amelia, dear?"

"Not a hatchling, but a juvenile old enough to fly. It's been flitting about the city and seems to be completely unattached."

Westing remembered the dragon they had encountered on their way into town. "No one knows where it came from?"

Lady Millicent leaned forward. "No, silly. That's why it's causing such an uproar. Everyone wonders what it means."

"It's been seen around the Tower, too," Lady Amelia added. "Its behavior is very odd. Unprecedented."

She gestured, and he saw it in the distance, gliding above the park like it was hunting. It appeared to be the same pale-yellow dragon he had encountered.

"You know, I'm making my debut this year," Lady Millicent said. "I hope I'll see you at the Queen's Drawing-room? And at the Dragon-linked Ball, of course."

"Perhaps," Westing said, trying to fob her off politely.

"I know dear Herbert would have been there."

Westing gritted his teeth at that, but his mind was drawn to the rogue dragon. He said his farewells to Lady Millicent and Lady Amelia and drove on.

He hated to admit it, but the rogue dragon's presence meant he should talk to Lord Blackerby again. As Home Secretary, Blackerby no doubt had someone who specialized in tracking dragons, and Westing did have information, scant though it might be.

Not on Lord Blackerby's terms, though. He would avoid the man's office. If he could catch him somewhere about town...

Lord Jasper's card party. Westing had intended to ignore the invitation, but it wasn't too late to send word that he would be there. Blackerby would be, too, thick as thieves with Jasper.

And the dragon lady might be there.

Westing shook the thought away. That made no difference. He was not going there to be social. He was going to meet Blackerby, and that would be the end of it.

Chapter Nine

WESTING HAD EXPECTED Lord Jasper's card party to be a small affair, so he was surprised when he had to squeeze through a crowd in search of Lord Blackerby. Most of the people in attendance were young ladies and gentlemen. The marriage mart was in full gallop. And several young ladies and their mamas turned hopeful eyes on him. He contained a sneer. They'd had no interest while his older brother was the prospective Lord Westing.

He would be expected to participate, though. He held out no hope for romance—his father and uncle had trained him well to understand that the warm and tender things in life were not meant for him—but he had a duty to his family name. Uncle Horace constantly reminded him of that. Westing's father had been conservative in his spending, so there was no pressure to hunt for an heiress, and Westing was dragon-linked, so he didn't need a lady with that distinction, either. But he would have to marry someone respectable beyond reproach, preferably from an old family.

Someone like Lady Millicent. He shuddered inwardly.

A group of young ladies fell into a fit of giggles when he walked past. He probably should be happy just to find a wife whose head wasn't filled with fluff. Enough time to worry about that in the future. He had heirs in Joshua and their younger sister Alexandra.

For now, he had business to attend to. Blackerby. The man wasn't in the house. Maybe he preferred the gathering night outside. Westing wound his way down to the garden.

Shadows trailed away from Blackerby like dark tendrils of fog, making him easy to find among the evergreen hedges. He was not, as Westing had expected, flirting with some notable lady, but instead engaged in a serious conversation with... was that one of the footmen?

When Blackerby noticed Westing, he dismissed the footman with a nod and turned to face Westing.

"Conspiring to turn Jasper's servants against him?" Westing asked.

Blackerby smiled. "Are you actually seeking me out, Westing? And here I thought we couldn't be friends." His voice was deep—almost too deep—but it always surprised Westing how normal Blackerby's eyes looked. Smart, sarcastic, but just an ordinary brown that did not hint at whatever secret knowledge the darkness made him privy to.

"I'm not here to be friends. I'm here to give you information."

"My favorite present. You want something in exchange, I suppose?"

The question brought Westing up short. Was this how Blackerby operated? "Just to be left in peace. Consider it a token of goodwill—that I will bring you information when I have it."

"I'm intrigued. Please, don't keep me waiting."

"The rogue dragon."

"I hope you have more than just its existence. Every child in London already knows that."

"But do you know where it comes from?"

Blackerby's eyes glittered with interest. "Do you?"

"Which direction, at least. It attacked me on the road from Dorset."

Blackerby swung his walking cane around, his eyes on the tip. "You're sure it's the same creature?"

"Are there many rogue dragons?"

"One must keep an open mind."

Westing sighed. "It looks the same. Same coloring. Rather small to be flying."

Blackerby twirled the cane again. "And you say it attacked you? What were you doing at the time?"

"Driving my curricle. My dragon and my brother were with me."

Blackerby tossed his cane up and caught it, looking into the distance thoughtfully. Staring into the shadows. What did they tell him? Westing shivered and decided not to wonder.

"Describe this attack."

"It followed us along the road for a short distance like it was looking for something. When it tried to land on the carriage, my dragon charged it. It swooped in on us, and my dragon fended it off. We left it beside the road."

"Its intention might not have been malicious, then," Blackerby mused. "But it showed an interest in you."

Blackerby studied him like a piece of bait, but Westing quickly put an end to that line of thought. "If it shows interest again, I will let you know, but when I drove my brother in Hyde Park today, it paid us no more heed than anyone else."

Blackerby clutched his cane and grinned. "Very strange. I do love a good mystery, don't you?"

"I will leave the mysteries to you," Westing said, bowing and turning to go.

"I have so many, though," Blackerby called to his back. "Like the Luddites. Do you hear much of them?"

Westing paused and faced him again. "You think the Luddites are connected to this rogue dragon?"

"They murdered Baron Ross."

"Rumor."

"Fact. The newspapers are not privy to all the knowledge I have. Baron Ross was stabbed with a lance—the symbol of St. George, slayer of the dragon who went mad and attacked the countryside. And the killer stole an opal button. Why?"

"Was it valuable? A family heirloom?"

"Apparently not. But people can be superstitious about opal. Think it brings good or ill fortune. Some even believe the light in opal comes from the mystical plane as dragon magic does. But I cannot make a connection."

"Lunatics sometimes keep mementos, do they not?"

"The kinds that do will kill again."

Westing's jaw tightened at that idea. "Then the rogue dragon's linked human may have been killed. Perhaps it is mad with grief."

"But who was that human, Westing? I am supposed to have records of all the linked dragons in England, but I do not know this one." Blackerby stared off into the night. "Do you have Luddite troubles at home?"

"Not in Dorset. Not many people use magic there."

"Yes, it's these northern upstarts, isn't it? A dragon-linked suddenly appears in their family, a throwback to some forgotten noble ancestor, they contract a brilliant marriage with a struggling lord's family, and then they bring their new ideas to old institutions. Using water magic to power mills or fire magic to smelt iron. Change frightens people."

"The changes have been small," Westing said. "Only a few eccentrics."

Blackerby looked into the distance as if he could see things far away. Perhaps he could. "Many small things can add up to large problems for a nation. Look at France." He scratched under his dragon's chin. "We do not want to end up like France."

"No." Not France, where anyone dragon-linked went to the guillotine, and their families, too, to cleanse the bloodlines. To be sure no magic lingered in the land, that no one had any unnatural advantage because of a link to the mysterious beasts. "If there were any way my abilities could serve England in the war—"

"No, no. We do not want to bring about another long winter, do we?" Blackerby regarded him curiously. "Does it not occur to you that you are more than just your attunement?"

Westing returned his steady gaze, trying to hide his confusion. "Of course."

"No, I don't think it does. No matter. You will understand someday. In the meantime, I hope you will keep your ear to the ground."

"For the dragon? Or the Luddites?"

"Yes."

"You're so certain they're related?"

"I fear it. The Luddites would see a guillotine set up outside the Tower, and the blood of us and our families staining the streets. You see, Westing, it is not I who threatens your loved ones."

Westing's stomach hardened into an icy knot. "You do plan to fight them, then?"

Blackerby raised his quizzing glass and looked at Westing through it. "Not if I can help it. I prefer to make them happy again. Fighting people causes them to be unhappy, and they fight even more. Happy people do not fight. Good evening, Westing."

Still chilled by the conversation, Westing accepted his dismissal. He walked back up the stairs to the card party in the ballroom, glad to put the darkness behind him.

The ballroom glowed beneath the candles in the chandelier

and the oil lamps on the walls. Guests played cards and gossiped as if there were no cares in all of England. No war boiling across the channel. No mysteries. It wasn't their concern, and it wasn't Westing's, either.

A figure caught his eye. Joshua's dragon lady. She did have a bit of gold in her hair, he decided—honey-colored highlights— and she looked much more respectable here than she had consorting on the streets with young boys and stray cats. Almost glowing as she studied the cards in her hand. But she was abominably rude. Ill-mannered. Improper.

"It's a shockingly sad state of affairs, is it not?" Lady Millicent asked in his ear.

"What's that?" Westing turned his attention reluctantly to the woman. She had snuck up on him.

"You know. Moving people out of their proper spheres. The skills of the dragon-linked are useful to the nation, so I understand why we might recruit them into the military." She giggled. "The men, of course. Don't look shocked." She swatted at him playfully, though he was certain he had not looked shocked. "But these vulgar country girls! It must be very uncomfortable for them to be placed where they don't belong. I don't know why we allow it."

He ignored her hand lingering on his arm. Instead, he considered what Blackerby had said. "I suppose it has something to do with their bloodlines."

"Perhaps. And I wish them well, of course." She looked into his eyes and practically purred, "But in the end, keeping the old bloodlines pure is sure to produce a better nation, don't you agree?"

She fluttered her eyelashes. He abominated such forced flirtation.

He moved his arm away. "What do you mean by pure?"

She turned far paler than any trick of face powder could have accomplished, obviously remembering the rest of his family. "Why, I meant coming of noble stock—used to positions of authority, regardless of what *nation* they might hail from. These peasants' children weren't born to it, were they?"

"The lady in question appears to be related to the Jaspers. I hardly expect her to be a peasant."

Lady Millicent waved her fan. "Ill-bred, though. I know, with your refined sensibility, you must see it. Like how she flaunts her magic. So crude!"

Indeed, the faint glow Westing had noticed around the lady had now resolved itself into sparkles of light. Oddly enough, she continued playing cards, apparently oblivious to the display she made of herself.

Chapter Ten

PHOEBE HAD the uncomfortable sense that everyone was staring at her, though she wasn't sure why. She tapped her foot. Perhaps it was because she was losing so badly to Lord Blanchfield, but the idea that people were whispering about her only made her play worse. She tapped her foot more rapidly.

When the hand was finished, Phoebe had lost again. She was just glad the ordeal was over. She felt like such a country fool.

"Another hand, Miss Hart?" Lord Blanchfield asked, almost leering at her.

Phoebe looked around for a means of saving herself the embarrassment, not to mention losing the last of the pin money her aunt had gifted her. Max would normally save her, but he had been lured to Bond Street to enjoy boxing and fencing with the Corinthian set, which he far prefered to card parties.

"Pardon me," said a female voice.

Phoebe looked up to see a tall, dark-skinned woman smiling at her. A purple dragon perched on her shoulder.

"We haven't been properly introduced," the woman said.

"I'm Eliza Prescott. Your aunt wished me to fetch you." Her smile looked a little too bright.

Was Deborah in trouble? Phoebe felt guilty leaving the girl alone upstairs, listening to a party she could not attend.

Phoebe rose and curtseyed to her partner. "Another time, my lord."

Eliza guided her away from Lord Blanchfield, who scowled in annoyance.

"Forgive my rudeness," Eliza whispered. "But I'm afraid you were being taken advantage of, and I couldn't bear to let it continue."

"Oh!" Phoebe flushed. Not Deborah, then. "No, it's just that I'm a very poor card player. My father doesn't care much for cards."

Eliza looked like she was restraining a smile, but she shook her head. "It's more than that, I'm afraid. Lord Blanchfield was being unscrupulous."

Phoebe's eyes widened, and she resisted the urge to look back. "He was cheating? But he's a lord!" Would her aunt invite such a scoundrel to her parties?

"He is the eldest son of the Earl of Greenley. Lord Blanchfield is only his courtesy title," Eliza said dismissively. "But even lords may be dishonorable, and you have a way of hinting if your hand is good or not."

"Oh, tapping my foot. I tried not to."

"No, it was... forgive my rudeness again, but are you attuned to light?"

"I am."

"You were, uh, rather sparkly when you had a good hand."

"Ah." Phoebe wished she could turn into a puddle and run down between the floorboards. Her face prickled with heat. Eliza looked sympathetic, which made Phoebe feel even worse. Perhaps they could put a rug over the floorboards after she had puddled between them, and people would forget she had ever come to London.

"I don't know how to stop it," she whispered.

Eliza considered her seriously. "You try to keep it hidden, then?"

"Wouldn't you? You can control your element, I suppose?"

"Well, yes. But my element isn't ever-present. I wonder if that makes it harder for you."

"It seems that everyone else's magic behaves."

Eliza looked thoughtful. "Come with me."

Phoebe let Eliza guide her, surprised the woman was willing to be seen in her company. But Eliza carried herself like a princess, completely unconcerned if people were staring at them. And people were. As if Phoebe had walked out of the house with her dress caught up in the back or something else vulnerable and terrible and unforgivable. And—heaven help her —Lady Millicent was there, staring at her and whispered to the horrid blond gentleman.

Eliza ignored them all and guided Phoebe down the stairs to the mezzanine overlooking the garden.

"Look at the man walking through the gardens," she said. "Don't stare, mind you; it wouldn't do to stare. But watch from the corner of your eye and pretend we are just talking."

Phoebe did as Eliza suggested. A tall gentleman paced the garden like a sentinel, apparently deep in thought. As he walked, the darkness trailed after him, a deep pool of black that followed like some strange, amorphous creature from the sea depths.

"He is… attuned to darkness?" Phoebe asked with a shiver. It had never occurred to her that if someone might be attuned to light, another might be attuned to darkness.

"Yes. That's the Earl of Blackerby. It's like that more after nightfall, but the darkness is always around him. And, I assure you, no one snickers at him."

"No! He's terrifying. And an Earl."

"Both may be factors. But consider, he's not ashamed of it."

"Oh." Phoebe was quiet for a long moment. "Where I come from, not many people were dragon-linked. I was always a bit of a..."

"A quiz?" Eliza asked with a grin. "In the West Indies, too! But, perhaps unlike in England, on Dominica, I could leverage it to my advantage. People were a little in awe. And now here I am, dancing with lords and snubbing their pretensions with a flick of my fan if I like."

Phoebe had not fully appreciated how much being dragon-linked was a ticket to doors that were normally closed firmly to any newcomers. But because the door was unlocked, did that mean she ought to go through it?

Eliza nodded as though guessing some of Phoebe's thoughts. "There will always be a few who will resent change, but don't let them cow you. Be proud of who you are, and most of them will fall into place."

"Thank you," Phoebe whispered. "I have been so nervous about the presentation."

"Oh, yes! I'm being presented this year, too. But as long as you can demonstrate your element, that will be enough. Don't be afraid."

Phoebe nodded, wishing she could snuff out fear like a candle. Her eyes fell on the gentleman with the white-blond hair, who was listening to Lady Millicent. It seemed that they had moved closer, as if it wasn't enough to mock Phoebe, but they also had to hound her.

Eliza sniffed and moved Phoebe out of their line of sight. "Now there's someone who won't like you no matter what you do."

Phoebe jumped. "Who?"

Eliza gurgled with laughter. "Lady Millicent Blanchfield, the sister of the gentleman who was fleecing you of your pin money.

She dislikes new blood excessively. Probably feels threatened by it. It brings me a thrill of pleasure to see her sour look every time I'm in the room with her."

Phoebe determined she would stay as far from any member of that family as possible. "And the gentleman she's flirting with?"

"I believe that's the new Viscount Westing, sixth of that title. Handsome, isn't he, in a formal way? He mostly keeps himself aloof. I don't think he likes anyone, not even Lady Millicent for all the lures she's throwing out to him. He's as unmoving as an iceberg." A servant passed with a tray of refreshments, and she took a glass of ratafia. "That's what he's attuned to, you know: ice. Do you think our elements influence our personality?"

Phoebe glanced in Lord Westing's direction and then at the figure of the Earl of Blackerby and shivered. "I don't know. What is your element, if I may ask?"

"Of course you may! It's water. Playful and free."

Phoebe smiled. "Well, maybe there's something to your idea." It occurred to her, though, that if she and Lady Millicent were both attuned to light, that must mean they had something in common.

She tilted her head to peek again at the icy Lord Westing, who now stood alone, frowning at the general assembly. He would be more handsome if he smiled, but he wore his black suit with easy elegance, his collar points starched but not so tall that they hid the strong line of his jaw. He caught her looking, and their eyes met. A jolt rushed through her at the connection, and she quickly looked away. What did it matter that the cold man didn't like her? Eliza seemed to argue that, if Phoebe didn't care, Mr. Westing couldn't hurt her. Nor Lady Millicent. She hoped Eliza was right.

"Thank you for… for your kindness, Miss Prescott," Phoebe said. "You have given me hope that I might not give myself up as an utter embarrassment."

"Of course you're not, Miss Hart. We newcomers ought to look out for each other."

"That you'll have to," said a male voice in the darkness, "if you're going to keep wandering off."

Phoebe gave a start, but Eliza only rolled her eyes.

"It gives me a moment of peace from you," she said.

A man stepped out of the shadows, and though Eliza seemed perfectly at ease with him, his appearance gave Phoebe a shock. He wore a patch over one eye and walked with a limp. His leg, she realized, was wooden. His face was handsome in a rough sort of way, but his face was tanned and his hair was bleached by the sun, as though he had spent a great deal of time at sea. A pirate! Or, were there still pirates anymore?

"Will you not introduce me to your lovely friend?" the man asked.

"I don't know if I wish to inflict that on her," Eliza replied.

"Now you're just being hurtful," he said with a grin full of rakish charm.

Eliza huffed. "Phoebe Hart, may I present Captain Parry to you? You ought to say no because he's a... a great lout!"

Captain Parry bowed to Phoebe. "She's only saying that because I won't let her buy a hat she particularly likes."

Eliza looked at Phoebe, her expression pained. "For reasons that escape me, my father thought Captain Parry would be a suitable guardian and executor for my funds while I was in London. It is most unfortunate."

"For both of us, love," he said ruefully.

"You are welcome to hand the management over to me." Eliza's eyes lit with hope.

"Then I truly would be a lout. Or at least a ninny."

"Come, Miss Hart," Eliza said loftily. "I believe I've had enough night air."

The captain chuckled as Eliza steered them to the doorway. Phoebe smacked into Lady Millicent, who lurked in the shadows of the curtain where she might have heard everything Phoebe and Eliza had said.

"Clumsy!" Lady Millicent gasped then smiled falsely. "A friendly hint, my dears. Learn to watch where you're going."

Lady Millicent's dragon hissed, and Mushroom growled in return. Several people in attendance turned to look at them. Phoebe's throat tightened. Was she about to make the night a perfect disaster?

Lady Amelia bumped into Lady Millicent, spilling her lemonade on Millicent's sleeve. "Oh, dear, I didn't see you there, Millie. What an odd corner to be standing in."

"My gown!" Millicent gasped.

Phoebe sighed and pulled out her handkerchief. "It is such a pretty fabric," she said, dabbing at the spot. "I do not think it will be ruined if you just—"

"Oh, do acquit yourself with more decorum! I want my maid. She will know how to care for it."

Lady Millicent glided off, leaving Phoebe bemused. At least no one was staring at her anymore, since their attention was on Lady Millicent. Lady Amelia gave her an arch smile and walked off. Had she done it on purpose?

"You are always trying to tame angry cats, it seems."

Phoebe whirled to find Lord Westing watching her, his expression impossible to read. She regarded him uncertainly. Was he trying to make a quiz of her? Mushroom hissed at Westing's dragon, which turned its back on them.

"The other cat was more friendly," Phoebe said cautiously.

"And more deserving of the help?" asked Lord Westing.

That sounded like a trap. "If so, you should have allowed your brother to pamper it."

"That would have made it a miserable creature."

Phoebe glanced to where Lady Millicent had departed. "I suppose misery does make us act our worst, doesn't it?"

Lord Westing's eyebrows drew together, and he made no response. Eliza took her arm and led her away.

"I warned you about them," Eliza whispered. "But I did not know you were acquainted with Lord Westing."

"Only… in passing."

"Still, you have spirit." Eliza smiled. "I predict your Season will be a success."

Phoebe hoped Eliza was right. She glanced back. Lord Westing watched her with a curious expression that she could not decipher.

Chapter Eleven

THE NEXT AFTERNOON, Phoebe retired to the library where she could avoid embarrassing herself in any way. She picked up a book her aunt had been reading. Her father often warned his daughters about the dangers of novels, but if Aunt Seraphina was reading it, it couldn't be *that* wicked. It contained tales of Prince Arthur and his knights. Only, Prince Arthur was an overweight, lecherous dandy who sent his men questing after a lost button, and she didn't find any of the familiar knights and ladies of his court—no Gawain, Kay, Lancelot, or Guinevere.

Except that Phoebe did recognize some of the characters. A dark-haired lady who smiled in people's faces but slipped strange potions in their food. A jester in a cloak of darkness. And a new arrival: a knight with white-blond hair who was slowly turning to stone.

Phoebe let out a sharp laugh of surprise. Someone was satirizing the *haut ton*. But who would dare?

She flipped over the book to find its author and was met by the obvious pseudonym Miss Charity. Someone who knew all the members of the *ton*, probably moved among them, but skewered them mercilessly on the page. Not charitable at all, but very daring. Prince Arthur must be the Prince Regent, and there was little favorable in his portrayal.

Miss Charity had favorites, though, and even the villains had sympathetic qualities. The dark-haired poisoner acted at the instigation of a cruel father. The jester was wise. Phoebe put her knuckles to her mouth when she recognized her aunt and uncle: a lovely but silly fairy trying to aid a bushy-eyebrowed knight so focused on duty that he did not notice as the fairy slowly faded to a shadow. It rang true, and it twisted Phoebe's heart.

Aunt Seraphina came into the room. "Oh, I see you've taken a fancy to Miss Charity's books!"

"Hmm. Do you enjoy them?"

"I often don't quite understand them, but they're all the rage."

"Really? Members of the *haut ton* enjoy them?"

"Oh, yes. I don't know why—the stories aren't the best I've seen—but I like being able to talk about them when I go visiting."

"Does anyone know who Miss Charity is?"

"No! That is the most exciting part. Everyone longs to know, but no one has any idea."

Wise of Miss Charity, Phoebe thought.

A shadow passed over the doorway. Phoebe jumped and set the book down. Her uncle walked in with Lord Blackerby and Lord Westing. Westing looked unenthusiastic about being there. He paused when he saw Phoebe, and some unreadable emotion flitted across his face. Was he still annoyed to find her in her aunt's home? Mushroom darted forward to bare his teeth at Westing's dragon, who flicked his tail and hissed in response.

"We need the room, dear," Lord Jasper said to Aunt Seraphina.

Phoebe stood quickly. It was clear they were discussing something important and the women's presence was unwanted.

But Aunt Seraphina seemed oblivious, only excited to see her husband.

"Did you see the strange advertisement in the paper?" her aunt asked.

Blackerby and Westing exchanged a look. Phoebe glanced at the newspaper her aunt displayed. There, in the personal advertisements, was a note in bold letters:

Where there is a dragon there must be a master. Submit peacefully or regret your folly.

"We saw," Blackerby said grimly. "That is what brought us to meet with your husband."

Aunt Seraphina's eyes widened. "You think it has something to do with the French? Or the Irish?"

Lord Jasper grimaced like he wanted to shoo his wife out of the room.

Blackerby, though, sat facing Aunt Seraphina and crossed one slender leg over the other. His dragon circled Phoebe, sniffing at her hem.

"I'm not sure," Blackerby said. "That is what concerns me."

"My dear," Lord Jasper said to Seraphina, gesturing to the door.

"Oh, of course! We'll be going." Aunt Seraphina motioned Phoebe out.

Phoebe took Miss Charity's book to show Deborah. Maybe the girl would recognize her mysterious aunt amid the caricatures. Mushroom snorted at Westing's dragon and trotted after her.

Max sat with Deborah in the antechamber, which was open enough to passersby in the corridor to keep it proper, considering the circumstances.

"You cannot be certain, then, the color of her hair?"

"It was not red, I'm positive," Deborah said with a self-assured nod.

Max gave Phoebe a desperate look. Still no luck getting any solid details about Aunt Janet-or-Jane. They knew she was not very tall or very short, her eyes were definitely blue or grey or—maybe—hazel or light brown, and she lived somewhere in London, either north of the Thames or south of it. But no red hair, evidently. Aunt Seraphina knew three Janes and one Janet, but all were deemed either too old or too young to be Deborah's aunt. Max was more than happy to gad about London talking to females, but even he needed more direction than this.

Phoebe sat next to Deborah. Mushroom, who was surprisingly respectful of the girl's fear, scampered to Max to butt his leg and demand a back scratch.

"What can you tell us about your mother?" Phoebe asked.

They had tried this tack before but only gleaned bits of information that didn't piece together to mean much.

Deborah turned her eyes to the plastered ceiling as she thought. "Oh! I do remember my father saying I looked like her."

"There, that's something," Phoebe said. "If your mother was blonde, your aunt is likely fair, too."

"Oh, yes, I imagine you are right! How delightful."

"You said her family did not approve of your father?" Phoebe prodded.

"I don't know if they didn't approve, but they did not get along. Father was very respectable. I cannot imagine anyone disapproving of him."

"Perhaps religious differences? Different backgrounds?"

Deborah wrinkled her forehead. "I don't know, and all this remembering is giving me a headache."

"Quite all right," Max said. "We know a little more now than we did. Is that a book you brought for Miss Sloan, Phoebs?"

"Yes, if she'd like."

"Thank you! That will be a lovely distraction." Deborah took the book, all signs of a headache gone.

Phoebe motioned with her head for Max to follow her into the corridor.

"I don't think she's trying very hard to remember this aunt of hers," she whispered once they were out of earshot.

"Think she made the woman up?"

"No. If she had, I believe she's creative enough to come up with more details."

Max chuckled. "Perhaps she just enjoys being restful. I suspect she's been hard used in the past."

Phoebe's merriment dimmed. She saw how Deborah flinched at sudden, loud noises. How she watched over her shoulder even in the safety of the antechamber. Those were not the fictions of an over-dramatic girl, no matter how imaginative she was. "I suppose it does no harm to keep her safe here for now. We don't even know that this aunt will treat her kindly."

"Just so. How do you plan to spend your evening? No more card playing for a time, I think."

"No, I've had my fill of that!" Phoebe shuddered. "I received a letter from Mama. I need to write back."

"With an edited version of your adventures thus far? You don't seem entirely happy here, Phoebs."

"It's an adjustment, but I don't want to go home just yet. I'll only dwell on the positives. They will want to hear all about the dressmaker."

Max held up a hand with an exaggerated grimace. "Save it for our sisters! I'll see if Miss Sloan can be distracted from her book long enough for a game of draughts."

Phoebe slipped into her room to fetch her letter. The days were short, and the room was already dusky. She concentrated, willing light to come to her.

Nothing.

She huffed and hummed a tune. At that, the light responded, flittering into existence and dancing around her head. The song was about a sparrow, and the light resolved itself into a little bird that soared around the room, trailing sparkles behind it. Phoebe gasped at the effect, completely out of her control, and the bird puffed out of existence.

Phoebe groaned and sat heavily at her dressing table. Mushroom put his foreclaws on her knees, blinking his black eyes as if in concern, then bounced over to curl up on the bed.

The bird would have been lovely for her presentation, but she had no idea if she would ever summon it back. And she couldn't summon anything without the help of a musical beat. She would have to have music at the drawing-room, and she suspected that was not common. She couldn't count on finding a pianoforte there. Her singing voice was only passable, at best, but with the addition of lights, maybe it would do.

She picked up the letter from her mother. It was cheerful, all about how well everyone was getting on. Kitty had a score of eligible suitors and would only have to choose from them. Everything was just wonderful. Without Phoebe.

But the party the previous night—everything in London— made it clear that this was no place for her either.

A tap sounded from the window, and Phoebe gave a start. Something moved outside on the balcony. She thought for a moment of the rogue dragon everyone gossiped about, but this was larger than that. Larger than a stray cat. Or even a dog.

She tucked the letter away and eased back toward the door, ready to call for help if needed. Then she watched. In a few moments, when she began to wonder if the maid would find her hiding in the dimness like a mad woman, the window creaked and swung open. Phoebe held her breath, but the housebreaker was so slight she could have imagined him to be a shadow.

A child.

The little thief snuck through the room, stopping to peer at her dressing table, but he did not take anything. He crept over toward the bed, and Mushroom raised his head with a growl.

The figure paused then let out a low breath, like a little sigh of amazement.

Phoebe stepped between the child and the window.

"Blimey!" The young boy spun around to face Phoebe. He glanced between her and the window and made a run for it.

He had not counted on Phoebe's many days in the woods with her brother, or the fact that she was an older sister used to wrestling noncompliant younger siblings. She tackled the struggling, shouting boy and hefted him over her shoulder then tromped into the hallway. Two maids and a footman were hurrying to her room, followed by Aunt Seraphina. Mushroom frolicked around them like a puppy looking forward to a game of fetch.

Max burst out of the antechamber. "Phoebe! What in blazes?"

A clammer of feet on the stairs announced more of the household: Lord Jasper, Lord Blackerby, but it was Lord Westing who led the way. He stopped short at the sight of her struggling with a disheveled street urchin.

"Put me down, put me down!" the boy screamed. "I'll bite you!"

"You will do no such thing," Phoebe said severely.

"You're 'andling me awful rough."

Phoebe swung him around and dropped him on the floor, not, however, letting go of his arm. "You broke into my room."

"He did what?" Westing asked, his voice hard.

The boy quailed.

"Don't frighten the child," she snapped at Westing. "Now," she said to the boy in a calm, big sister voice, "It could not have been easy to climb to my window."

The boy's sniveling calmed a little at that. "It warn't easy at all, miss."

"Then why did you do it?"

"A man said 'e'd pay me if I did."

"Were you to take anything?" Lord Jasper demanded.

The boy pinched his lips together, but Phoebe said, "It's no use, you see. We've caught you. Now, what was the man going to pay you for breaking in?"

"A shilling."

"Very well. I will give you two if you tell me who sent you and why."

"Really?" The boy's eyes lit up.

"On my honor."

"Sounds alright by me. I don't know who the bloke was. Kept 'is face covered. But 'e wore rum togs like a real swell."

"Is he still outside?" Blackerby asked.

"No, 'e said 'e would find me."

"Fair enough," Phoebe said. "And why did this, er, 'swell' wish you to break into my room? Was it my room specifically?"

"It was. 'E wanted to know everything I could find out about the dragon lady in this 'ouse. That's you, ain't it?"

"Indeed, it is. How odd. He didn't ask you to take anything?"

"No, miss. Just wanted me to poke about your room, tell 'im what I saw. I 'ave an excellent memory, you see. Other men— those what ain't gentlemen—they sometimes 'ave me tell them the 'abits of certain 'ouseholds."

"I see," Phoebe said. "What an interesting talent that they are putting to bad use."

"Did he ask about jewelry?" Blackerby asked. "Fallalls, fawneys, other moveables?"

"Just what sort the lady seemed to like."

"Opals?" Blackerby asked with studied indifference.

"I don't know opals, sir. They shiny?"

Phoebe watched Blackerby's face, but he gave nothing away. The dragon-linked baron had been killed for an opal button, but there were any number of nefarious reasons a criminal might wish to know what jewelry she had. Still, she resolved not to wear her mother's opal bracelet.

"Ought to turn him in," Max said, glaring at the boy.

Aunt Seraphina, who had watched with wide eyes, said, "Oh, must we, do you think? He's only a child. Not even a very big one."

Lord Jasper frowned. "If his criminal ways aren't—"

"Wait," Phoebe interrupted. "What's your name, young man?"

"Jamie," he said. "Brainy Jamie, they call me."

"Well, Jamie, we are not going to turn you over to the constables."

"Oh, thank you, miss!"

"We're not?" Lord Jasper asked.

Phoebe forced a smile in the face of her uncle and his intimidating eyebrows. "No, sir, we are not. In fact, Jamie, we are going to give you a warm meal and three shillings, and then we are going to send you out to tell tales to the man who sent you in."

"Phoebs!" Max protested.

"No, I see it," Blackerby said with a smile. "Miss Hart is recruiting him."

"Doing what now?" Brainy Jamie asked.

"What he means," Phoebe said, "is that you can go back to that man and tell him what my room was like. I can't think of any harm in that. You can even tell him I own pearls—every young lady does. If he asks you to do anything else, you'll report it to me."

"And I'll get another shilling?"

"And a warm meal whenever you need one. We'll tell the girls in the kitchen not to turn you away."

"And I can keep 'is shilling, too?"

"Of course. But you must not tell him about our agreement."

"Course not!" Jamie grinned.

"Then we'd best get you to the kitchen for a quick bite and have you back out the window before he gets suspicious."

"Yes, miss!" The boy skipped happily after a dubious maid to find the kitchen.

"Very clever, Miss Hart," Blackerby said, feigning a slow handclap.

"I hope so," Lord Jasper said. "To think of someone breaking into this house—"

"And to Phoebe's chambers!" Aunt Seraphina said. "I can't understand why anyone would want to know about them. It seems very vulgar."

"No doubt it is," Westing said.

"I've never heard of a suitor going to such lengths," Aunt Seraphina said. "Or could it have to do with the presentations? One of the other ladies trying to get an advantage?"

"That would be quite shocking," Blackerby said. "I like the devious turn of your mind."

Aunt Seraphina reddened and looked pleased.

Phoebe thought of Lady Millicent but shook her head. "No, it makes no sense. I am not so threatening to anyone else's success, and little could be gained from knowing the content of my rooms. I think there is some other mystery here, and young Jamie is our only connection to it."

"But Phoebs!" Max cried. "You promised. No urchins."

"I promised no such thing," she reminded her brother.

He groaned and rubbed his eyes. Phoebe's uncle watched her with suspicion, Blackerby smiled in approbation, and Westing's face remained unreadable.

A warning flared in Phoebe's mind that it might be safer to go home after all, but she was not so weak-spirited that she would run away from a mystery or a boy in need of being rescued from the streets.

Chapter Twelve

WESTING WAS BEING DRAWN IN. Blackerby—blast him!—had Westing entangled in the affair of the rogue dragon and possibly Baron Ross's murder. And Miss Phoebe Hart...

She probably didn't notice if Westing were alive or dead. But she had drawn him in, too. She was inexplicably kind to Lady Millicent, even after the woman had been so sneering to her. And taking in a street urchin to act as her spy? It was just the sort of strange, bold thing he would expect from a girl who helped boys climb trees, unleashed her biting tongue on anyone she disagreed with, and generally had no notion of how to behave properly. And he couldn't stop thinking about her.

He picked up the family seal, staring at the heavy, rigid brass. Duty first. If he was honest with himself, Miss Hart's behavior shamed him a little, too. She was generous in a way he didn't understand. His father would have disapproved of the lady, and Horace would despise her, but Westing could not.

"West?"

Joshua's voice brought him back to the library. The boy watched him uncertainly. Westing was scowling again, so he tried to soften his face. The way Miss Hart had softened hers dealing with Brainy Jamie. He set the seal down on his right. "What is it, Joshua?"

He hoped he didn't sound too snippy.

"Mr. Sudbury has gone. He says my Latin is progressing well, but I ought to know more geography. I'm studying the atlas, but I wanted to know if we might get a chance to see anything today?"

Westing almost told his brother he was too busy, but in truth, he was only busy brooding. A sorry excuse. "I assume you don't mean a tour of the Continent. Napoleon won't allow it."

"Of course not, sir," Joshua said, clearly not understanding that he was teasing.

"What did you have in mind?"

"Fireworks?"

"I don't know of any fireworks planned for tonight."

"I saw in the paper that there's some kind of grand celebration coming up in a couple of days."

"Ah, that would be the Queen's Drawing-room for the new dragon-linked ladies making their debut and the ball after."

"Is my… the dragon lady going to be there?"

"Her name, I have learned, is Miss Hart, and she will be there, but you will not. You are too young to go to court." Seeing Joshua's disappointment, he quickly added, "But you are not too young to visit the Tower of London."

"Isn't that where they put famous prisoners?"

Westing laughed. "Is there a prisoner you'd like to see?"

Joshua shrugged. "Just something interesting. Not much happens on the square. I did see a lady lose her umbrella and chase it all over the park until a gentleman caught it for her."

"Not first-rate entertainment. But the tower has a royal menagerie with wild animals on display. It's also rumored to be the home of the oldest dragon in England."

"Is it huge? Can we see it?"

"They say it sleeps beneath the tower, ready to defend England in her hour of greatest need."

"Like King Arthur!"

"Indeed. This dragon—the White Dragon of England—is supposed to have been the mate of his Red Dragon of Wales."

"Ooo!"

"There's nothing of it to see, though, except the great rise in the earth where it rests."

"I still want to visit."

"Very well. We shall."

Westing glanced at the family seal again. It looked odd there, not where his father always placed it. Westing left it and called for his curricle.

They rode through London, Joshua nearly bouncing on the seat while Westing pointed out the Inns of Court, St. Paul's Cathedral, and London Bridge on the way to the Tower. This was good for the boy's education, wasn't it? What else did Westing need to do to care for his brother—to keep Horace off his back and make amends for his past mistakes? Ensure that the boy had an honorable profession. His missing hand precluded him from the military. Maybe he would do well in the Church.

Crowds thronged the Tower—patrician and plebeian alike. Westing turned the curricle over to his groom and placed a hand on Joshua's shoulder to keep him close. Dragon watched the milling mass of humanity from his perch on Westing's shoulder.

Joshua led Westing to the cages with wolves, bears, ostriches, and even a tigress. Joshua's eyes brightened with wonder, and Westing had to pull him back to keep him from petting the tigress's foot through the bars. But Westing pitied the animals. Cooped up in cages, fed garbage by onlookers, and destined to live out their lives trapped in London.

Finally, he'd had a stomach full of it and beckoned Joshua over to see the dragon mound next to the White Tower. The

Tower ravens flocked about, hopping over the ground, secure in their knowledge that no one would disturb them.

"They keep the dragon's secrets," Westing informed Joshua, "and tell it what's going on all over Britain. Maybe even deliver messages between it and the Red Dragon in Wales."

Joshua stared at Westing's dragon, who had glided down to watch the ravens. "Dragons can talk?"

"Not young ones, but some stories say the adults can."

They gazed over the mound. There was a local hill near Westing's estate that was supposed to be the hibernation site of a lesser dragon, but the entire hill that held the White Tower was magnificent, looking out over the Thames as it made its sluggish way past.

A commotion of gasps and hollers behind them drew Westing's attention. The rogue dragon had returned. Lady Amelia had mentioned that it frequented the Tower. It flapped down to land among the ravens. They didn't scatter but milled around the creature like they were welcoming a member of their flock. Maybe they could communicate with this dragon, too, but what message were they sharing?

The scarcely-muted whispers continued, but another noise caught Westing's attention. A deep rumble, almost too low to hear—it vibrated through his legs. Slowly, the other visitors to the Tower became aware of it, too, and they all grew quiet.

The animals, however, squawked and roared. Westing covered his ears, and Joshua wobbled a little as if his legs were unsteady beneath him.

Then, all at once, it went still.

Westing lowered his hands and looked around. Everyone seemed stunned.

"Well," said a voice behind Westing. "That was quite a show."

Westing turned to find Blackerby strolling up behind him, walking cane in hand.

"I suppose I shouldn't be surprised to see you here," Westing said.

"No, you shouldn't be. I have people watching the Tower to inform me when our little rogue friend appears." He took a pinch of snuff. "This, however, is the first time it has elicited a reaction from the beast below. At least we know our guardian angel is still alive down there."

"Dragons can't die," Joshua said.

Blackerby raised an eyebrow at him. "No one thinks they can. But that does not mean they are correct."

"What would happen if the White Dragon did die?" Joshua asked, eyes wide.

Westing thought Blackerby would dismiss the boy's question, but the earl leveled a serious look at him. "You are asking about a hypothetical situation. I do have a man studying such questions. He posits that hibernating dragons contribute to keeping their element healthy. Since the White Dragon is, according to legend, the heart and soul of England, its death would mean the ruin of our nation."

"Oh," Joshua said quietly. "Then I hope it cannot die."

"As do I," Blackerby said, but his forehead was creased in worry when he looked back to the dragon's hill.

"You think it a real possibility?" Westing asked quietly, glancing around to be sure they were not overheard.

"I think this little dragon is drawn to its enormous cousin for a reason. I hope it is not here as a replacement. It does not inspire confidence."

Westing glanced back at the small, pale-colored dragon fluttering about with the ravens. "No, it does not."

"Furthermore, our dragon-linked king is struck with a mysterious affliction," Blackerby said. "His mind is too disordered to rule. And his dragon is ill. Has your dragon ever been ill?"

"Never."

"Precisely. It's unheard of." Blackerby paced. "And we have the Luddites rising. They murdered Baron Ross, at least. I don't know if any of it is connected, but it worries me how little we understand."

Westing wanted to convince himself that none of this was his concern. Joshua's movement caught his eye. The boy was trying to sneak closer to the rogue dragon, reaching out with his one good hand, though the creature was wise enough to keep its distance. If the nation was in danger, so were the people Westing cared about, and protecting his family was definitely his concern.

"I suppose I will see you at the Queen's Drawing-room for the dragon-linked ladies," Blackerby said.

Westing shot him a sideways glance. "I had not planned on going."

"It shows the dragon-linked women that they are welcome in our society. Creates a sense of connection. Especially for those not born into the ranks of nobility."

Westing suppressed a groan. He didn't know how welcome they were by the likes of Lady Millicent, but he didn't wish the ladies ill.

"Oh, that means you'll see the pretty dragon lady again, won't you?" Joshua asked, bounding over. "Miss Hart?"

Blackerby raised an eyebrow at Westing and smirked. "Indeed, lad, he will."

Chapter Thirteen

PHOEBE COULDN'T SLEEP the night before the Queen's Drawing-room. She paced her chamber, practicing songs that helped her magic manifest. Each time she sang, the effect was different. She might get spinning orbs that burst into a shower of butterflies or a faint sparkle that fizzled away. And after wearing out her voice in experiments, she sounded raspy when dawn broke—not promising.

It took most of the morning and two maids to get her dressed. Mrs. Reynolds had delivered a gown that was certainly… noticeable. With the huge white skirts and little spangles reflecting the light, Phoebe felt like a chandelier. She practiced her curtsey to be sure she wouldn't fall over. Mushroom darted around her skirts trying to steal the spangles.

"You can have them all when this is over," she promised the dragon, scooping him up and giving him a string of paste diamonds to keep him distracted.

By the time Aunt Seraphina called for the carriage, Phoebe was light-headed from lack of sleep and food, her appetite having vanished.

Aunt Seraphina had a hooped court dress as well, though hers was a restrained blue. They barely squeezed all their fabric and hooping into the carriage. Phoebe had to keep her head low to avoid damaging the required ostrich feathers crowning the costume.

When the carriage pulled up to Buckingham Palace, Phoebe was afraid the hoops would fling her out like a toy on a spring, but she managed to descend with relative grace thanks to the help of two footmen.

It helped her spirits—a little—that everyone else wore the same ridiculous gowns. And Mrs. Reynolds had been right to keep the waist unfashionably low. Some of the women with high waists looked like they wore hot-air balloons under their skirts, ready to swallow them and float away.

Phoebe and Aunt Seraphina were guided through a blur of magnificent rooms that left Phoebe speechless. Paintings and columns and crystals in the chandeliers—she put a hand on Mushroom to be sure he stayed right where he belonged. She had to maneuver through crowds of people, many of whom had dragons as well, and she kept forgetting her hoop and apologizing when she bumped someone.

The young ladies being presented stood out for their white dresses. There were only a few, but this drawing-room was particularly for those who were dragon-linked. She spotted Eliza across the room. She was tall enough to almost make the hoops look elegant, and the white dress set off her golden-brown skin and dark hair. The way she mingled with the highest members of the court, one wouldn't know she had spent most of her life far off in the West Indies. Phoebe, on the other hand, felt like a child at a costume ball. She was grateful when Eliza shot her a friendly smile.

Being presented to the queen was the least frightening part of the ordeal. Phoebe curtseyed deeply without falling over and kissed Queen Charlotte's hand. The grand lady smiled on her, and Phoebe backed away. Then the next lady had her turn, and that part was over.

Phoebe's breath felt a little shaky, but she smiled in relief.

"You did very well, dear," Aunt Seraphina whispered.

"Thank you." Phoebe glanced around the room. "Next, the hard part."

The crowds cleared to the edges of the huge drawing-room with the ladies who were to demonstrate their abilities gathered on one side. Besides Eliza and Lady Millicent, two other young ladies looked serene in their white dresses. Phoebe's hands felt clammy, but she tried to take deep breaths and not give away her terror.

Eliza sidled up to her. "Are you ready?"

"Probably not. I don't understand how everyone else seems so calm."

There were certainly enough important people in the room. In addition to Her Majesty, the Prince Regent with his plump red dragon sitting beside him, and several of the Royal Dukes, she spotted Lord Westing and Lord Blackerby among the crowd, but everyone seemed more interested in gossiping and gowns than the displays of attunement.

"They see this every year," Eliza reminded her.

Eliza was the first one summoned to perform. She called for two glasses of water to be brought before her. Liveried footmen set up the table. Eliza paused dramatically, then gestured over them. The water swirled in the glasses, forming small waterspouts. The waterspouts grew until they met in the middle. The water shot up into the air, then rained back down. Before they hit the table, Eliza waved her hand, and the droplets separated back into the two glasses.

Polite clapping echoed around the room, and Eliza curtseyed. The onlookers seemed almost bored. Phoebe couldn't imagine how they had become so jaded. She marveled at how easy it looked for Eliza, as though she were just pouring tea and not commanding the elements to bend to her will.

The next lady, attuned to fire, lit a whole series of candles in a chandelier just by touching them. A young woman attuned to air played a pretty song on a wind-chime. Phoebe perked up at that. Could she have another instrument brought in? Glancing around, she realized the drawing-room opened on a music room, and she spotted a pianoforte. Relief poured over her shoulders like the warmth of sunshine.

"Lady Millicent Blanchfield."

Phoebe drew a deep breath and held it, waiting to see what she had to compete with.

Lady Millicent stepped to the center of the room. Her dragon followed after and settled beside her hooped skirt. Ladies fanned themselves, keeping stiff, polite smiles as Lady Millicent curtseyed and then held her hand gracefully in the air. Little floating orbs of light appeared near the ceiling one at a time, illuminating the room in a glow almost as bright as noonday. Then they all blinked out at once. Phoebe wished that she could control her abilities with such ease. Lady Millicent curtseyed again, and the audience clapped dully.

Eliza wore a look of exaggerated boredom.

"That's very practical," Phoebe whispered to her. "I wonder if it could be used in a greenhouse."

Eliza gave her an incredulous look. "You think Lady Millicent has ever set foot in a greenhouse?"

"Miss Phoebe Hart."

The room grew quiet, and all eyes turned to Phoebe. Lady Millicent smirked at her. Had someone deliberately set the stage so she, with the same attunement as Millicent, would have to perform directly after her? Her face warmed, but she walked forward, past the opening in the center of the room to the pianoforte just visible in the next one.

A few people murmured or snickered, but Phoebe

remembered what Eliza had said about not being cowed and continued deliberately on. Lord Westing appeared at her side.

"I think you misunderstand, Miss Hart," he whispered urgently. "You are not to perform music. You are expected to display your magic."

Her face flamed. What a scene he was making, and her heart was already beating so fast it felt like it would flutter away. "I think *you* misunderstand, my lord."

Forgetting her nerves in a rush of irritation, Phoebe pushed past him and stopped in front of the piano. She didn't know if she could perch on the bench without her hoops flipping up, and she was not supposed to sit in the queen's presence anyway. She stood and ran her fingers up the smooth ivory keys in a tripping scale.

Dragonflies made of light danced away from the piano-forte. Several swirled around Westing's head and then popped out of existence, ringing him in a halo of twinkles.

Someone in the room tittered at Westing's look of surprise. Eliza perhaps? Otherwise, the drawing-room had gone completely quiet. Mushroom curled up on the top of the pianoforte and watched Phoebe expectantly. She took a deep breath and started in on her favorite sonata from Beethoven.

As her fingers danced over the haunting minor notes of the song, ghostly figures of light formed over the piano, wavering and fluttering in time with the music like the northern lights on a cold winter night. Phoebe lost herself in the steady downbeats of the song, swaying in time with the rhythm, but she could sense the lights glowing around her and the utter silence in the room.

Concerned that her audience would grow bored, Phoebe jumped ahead to the rapid notes of the third movement. As she pounded the keys, horses of light pranced around the room. A gentleman cried out in surprise, and a few of the ladies gasped. Phoebe glanced up, worried she was going too far, but Eliza gave her a reassuring nod. Too late to stop now. Phoebe played on. The horses danced and leaped on the air, trailing glimmers of light behind them until she came to the final chords and folded her hands in front of her.

She glanced up in time to see the last flickers of the horses disappear. The audience stared at her. Her face heated, and she looked down at her fingers. Now she had made a shocking display of herself, and everyone would say she was a forward girl.

Applause started slowly, scattered here and there, but then it built to a roar. Phoebe looked up in surprise to see most of the people smiling and clapping enthusiastically. The Prince Regent. The Queen. She remembered herself and curtseyed. As she did, she caught the look Lady Millicent gave her, full of spite.

Phoebe quickly retreated to Eliza's side.

"They liked it?" Phoebe asked quietly.

"You put the rest of us to shame," Eliza said with a grin. "And look who noticed."

Lord Blackerby strolled toward them, dark mists trailing behind his feet. He stopped and bowed crisply to Eliza and Phoebe.

"Miss Hart, Miss Prescott. I hope I may have the pleasure of dancing with each of you tonight. I assume you are attending the Dragon-linked Ball. Not a formal requirement, but everyone will expect to see you there."

Phoebe nodded, her mouth dry. All eyes were on her. And not all of them were friendly.

Phoebe was allowed a brief rest after the Queen's Drawing-room and was then once again dumped into the merciless hands of her aunt's lady's maid to dress her and restyle her hair. Mrs. Reynolds had produced a ball gown reminiscent of Phoebe's court gown—white with gold spangles—and Phoebe was laced into it and decorated with a simple pearl necklace and earrings. She managed to eat a little bread and cheese before her aunt packed her back into the carriage.

The Dragon-linked Ball was held at the Prince Regent's Carlton House on Pall Mall. The outside of the grand, colonnaded building was lit with floating magic baubles, and before it stood a fountain that did tricks with water and colors throughout the night as well as a miniature model of London with tiny carriages that moved through the streets on their own. Phoebe couldn't decide if the last was magic or mechanics, but she was delighted by its detail.

"What is the Prince Regent attuned to?" Phoebe asked her aunt.

"Earth," her aunt whispered. "Like our poor king. They rarely demonstrate their magic, though, even when His Majesty is well."

Phoebe imagined such a demonstration could have very damaging consequences.

The ballroom was a crush, but somehow the crowds let Phoebe through. Her face heated as people who were not present at the Queen's Drawing-room whispered and stared.

It did not help when Lord Blackerby came forward to claim his dance.

"Do you waltz?" he asked.

"I learned, but I am not sure it's proper." Phoebe's father had been very skeptical of a dance that allowed a man and woman to stand so close and twirl about the room.

"If you are dancing it with me, it is."

Blackerby led her to the floor and took her arms. Phoebe was all too conscious of the darkness swirling on the ground beneath their feet.

"The shadows will not hurt you, dear." He smiled, almost sincerely. "No more than your baubles of light will hurt me."

She glanced up. Sparkles twinkled around their heads. Phoebe wanted to bury her face in her hands and flee, but Blackerby held her still.

"Darkness and light, eh, Miss Hart?"

"I— I cannot help it, my lord. It's the music—"

He cocked his head. "Music helps you control your magic?"

"But sometimes, when there's a rhythm, I cannot help it."

"Fascinating. You don't have to let that be common knowledge."

"They will think I'm showing off."

"And why shouldn't you? You reminded them of what magic can be."

"Parlor tricks," Phoebe murmured.

"It may seem so. But at least yours was not dull."

She caught herself nodding.

"Yes, you thought it unimpressive, too? Water, fire, light, wind. They might have better uses than making the drawing-room pretty. Those ladies did things that could just as easily have been done with household objects, with the possible exception of Miss Prescott. You, however—nothing but magic could have done what you did. It was delightful."

"Easy for a man to say. Women are not supposed to draw so much attention to themselves."

"Miss Prescott might disagree."

They glanced over to where Eliza was entertaining a group of admiring young men by making the lemonade dance in her glass. Her protective Captain Parry stood to the side, his eye patch incongruous with his formal attire.

"This is why new blood is good for us," Blackerby said. "There's something in the Bible, is there not, about hiding one's light?"

Phoebe chewed over that thought long after Blackerby had delivered her back to her aunt and other men had come forward to ask her to dance. Whatever dark looks some people might be giving her, several of the gentlemen found her interesting. Novel, at least. Not an embarrassment. There might be some hope for her in London after all.

She stepped away during a break in the music to sip a lemonade and cool her flushed cheeks. Stepping to an open window, she almost collided with Lord Westing. Had he been watching for her?

He waited for her to acknowledge him, though they had never been properly introduced, so she could cut him without a second thought. He had nearly ruined her performance and humiliated her. Now, he watched her with those hard-to-read blue eyes that almost matched the color of his waistcoat and the dragon perched on his shoulder. Of course, someone so well-bred would manage to have a dragon that coordinated with his eyes.

"Lord Westing," she said, barely inclining her head.

He bowed. "Miss Hart." After a long pause, he added, "Are you free? For a dance?"

Phoebe raised an eyebrow. "You wish to dance with me?"

His lips quirked. "That is why I asked." He cleared his throat. "I was wrong. At the Queen's Drawing-room. I thought you didn't understand, but I see that I was the one who did not. I would like to make peace with you. Besides." He smiled. "My brother often asks if I've spoken to you. After refusing him a cat, I would hate to disappoint him in this."

He offered his hand.

Phoebe hesitated. This might be a new way of teasing her. His jaw had a stubborn set to it. It was also faintly stubbled, and she had a wicked curiosity to know if it would tickle if she ran her fingers over it. She set her lemonade aside and laid her hand in his.

Westing led her out for another waltz. His fingers were chilly, and she wondered if he did not have perfect control over his magic either. But soon, the only thing she was aware of was his closeness. The way her pulse beat much faster than the rhythm of the music. She felt too shy to meet his eyes, instead studying the fit of his waistcoat across his broad chest. He didn't speak either, even when little stars of light appeared above them.

The dance ended, and they stood for a moment, neither letting go. Then Westing slowly released her hand and bowed.

Aunt Seraphina shepherded her through the rest of the ball, one long blur of dances, but when Phoebe returned home and collapsed into sleep, the song that played in her dreams was a waltz.

Chapter Fourteen

"TELL ME EVERYTHING ABOUT COURT. And the ball! Did you actually *waltz*?" Deborah leaned over the breakfast tray in the sitting-room, her face glowing with interest.

Max rolled his eyes and swung his newly-acquired quizzing glass on its chain, but he also looked curious about Phoebe's debut.

Phoebe gave them a brief account of the day with enough details to satisfy Deborah's imagination but not bore her brother too much. She hesitated, then admitted to Deborah her difficulty with her magic and her luck at finding the pianoforte.

Max grinned. "I would have liked to see that. Imagine you making some gentleman shriek."

But Deborah cast a nervous glance at Mushroom, who was devouring a sausage beside the breakfast tray. "Is it common for dragon-linked people to have trouble controlling their magic? It must be frightfully dangerous." She looked toward the ceiling as though expecting a magical cataclysm to crash upon them.

"I don't think it is common," Phoebe admitted. "At least, you don't see people going around catching things on fire or causing hurricanes. Though maybe most people don't have magic that strong. The lady who was attuned to fire only lit some candles."

"Lord Blackerby always has those shadows about him," Max said.

Phoebe remembered dancing with darkness swirling on the floor beneath her feet. "That might be on purpose."

"It seems rather devilish," Deborah said with a shudder.

Phoebe suspected Deborah thought all magic was devilish. She might be a Luddite. Not a harmful one but reared on their philosophies. It made Phoebe less enthusiastic about turning her over to the mysterious aunt, who might belong to that sect.

When Phoebe descended the stairs later, she found her aunt in rapture over several large bouquets in the front hall.

"My dear, you have arrived!" Aunt Seraphina beckoned her over. "You shall have your voucher for Almack's despite your waltz with Lord Blackerby."

"Was it wrong?" Phoebe asked, horrified. "He told me it was not."

"He may do what he likes, but it was very bold for a girl newly launched in society to waltz. Never mind that, though. It worked to your advantage. Look at what your admirers have sent!"

Phoebe stared at all the flowers, cards, and invitations her aunt laid before her. "These are all for me?"

"Indeed! So many requests to perform at musicales—I hope your fingers don't tire easily!—and several invitations to exclusive balls as well. You are a most sought-out guest."

Warmth spread over Phoebe's skin—relief mingled with excitement and nervousness. She had hoped to not make a fool of herself. She had never expected to be feted. She touched the cards that came with the flowers. White lilies from Lord Blackerby—that seemed safe enough. Roses with a note in French. Huge yellow daisies from a Sir Francis. Nothing from Lord Westing. Not that she had expected anything.

"You will make your appearance at Almack's as soon as possible, of course," Aunt Seraphina was saying. "You may find it a little dull—the Lady Patronesses are so strict—but it will let the *ton* know that you are acceptable."

"Available," Phoebe whispered.

"What's that, dear?"

"It will let them know I'm on the marriage mart, won't it?"

"Naturally, though that is a crude way for a young lady to express it."

"I'm sorry," she said automatically.

"I'm sure we can expect you to start receiving callers soon."

Phoebe's stomach tripped itself into knots. Men dancing with her, sending her flowers, courting her. This was why she came to London. To find her place. And now she was terrified. How was she to know which men might make good husbands? What if she didn't like any of them? She was not wealthy, so she didn't have to worry about fortune hunters, but she also didn't want to be married to someone just because she had a dragon and was a novelty.

Max would have to help her by finding out which were gamblers or drunks or libertines—the sort of thing no one would tell a young lady, though she had the most need to know. Or Phoebe could send her little spy, Brainy Jamie. She stifled a giggle at the thought. He made occasional appearances in Grosvenor Street to tell her he had not seen the strange man again and then eat himself sick in the kitchen.

Aunt Seraphina did not allow Phoebe much time to worry. She ordered her lady's maid to see which dress would be best for Almack's, how her hair ought to be done, and if they needed to order anything else from Mrs. Reynolds. Her aunt coached her on all the rules of the exclusive Almack's, drilling her until she did not have room in her mind for much else. This, Phoebe decided, was how most ladies must survive the whirl of the Season—by not giving themselves time to think.

The next Wednesday, her aunt escorted her to the august halls of Almack's Assembly Rooms. They arrived in good time, well before the doors were closed to all comers for the night. Phoebe felt much less silly in the light-yellow silk gown Mrs. Reynolds had made for her than she had in her court dress. Mushroom sat on her shoulder, peering about with interest at the other dragons. They entered the ballroom with its glittering chandeliers and mirrors, the occupants' jewelry and quizzing glasses glinting in the light.

"Please don't steal anything," Phoebe whispered to the dragon.

The Lady Patronesses were wise, however, and as well as bland refreshments, they also offered trays of trinkets to keep dragons amused. Phoebe smiled and offered Mushroom a string of glass beads. Perhaps he wasn't so naughty after all—no worse than any other young dragon.

There were so many fine ladies and gentlemen that Phoebe expected to be completely lost in the crowd. Lady Millicent cut Phoebe, turning her back on her. But, as at the Dragon-linked Ball, young men sought Phoebe out to dance. Not the waltz, which the Patronesses turned their noses up at, but she was grateful. The country dances she had practiced so faithfully were much more comfortable.

When she escaped her partners for a drink of orgeat, she encountered Eliza Prescott sipping from a glass, her eyes bright with enjoyment. Eliza's purple dragon made a friendly chuffing noise at Mushroom, who bobbed his head in return.

Eliza smiled. "It appears we are to be embraced by our peers here in Almack's hallowed halls."

"Indeed, though..." Phoebe stopped herself from saying anything rude about the assembly.

Eliza tilted her head confidentially. "It's not very exciting, is it?"

"I admit it feels..." she couldn't find the words. Empty. Like something was missing.

"Perhaps the Patronesses are a trifle too exacting," Eliza whispered. "But at least here I am safe from the oversight of Captain Parry."

"Oh, is it because he is... is it because of his leg or his eye?"

Eliza laughed. "I suspect it's because he doesn't care a fig for their rules. Though his wooden leg is probably not up to their standards of dress, never mind that he earned it sailing against the French."

Phoebe detected a hint of bitterness in Eliza's tone and wondered if her new friend was truly so glad to be rid of Captain Parry.

A slim, good-looking gentleman bowed to both ladies and addressed Phoebe with a heavy French accent. "Would Miss Hart honor me with the next dance?"

"Of course, Mr... um..." She looked to Eliza for help, but her friend could only offer her an amused smile and a shrug.

"Moreau," the man said. "Pierre Moreau. Alas, I should have known I would be forgotten in so large a crowd of admirers. We danced the quadrille at the Dragon-linked Ball."

"Oh! I am so sorry." A vague memory surfaced from the rush of the ball's exhaustion, nerves, and excitement. "I believe I owe you thanks for the lovely roses. I do remember you, only I could not recall your name. Forgive me."

"When you smile like that, all is forgiven."

Phoebe chuckled. "I suspect you are a flirt."

"*Oui.* I am French." He grinned, winked at Eliza, and offered Phoebe his arm.

"How do you like England?" Phoebe asked as they danced in their set.

"The climate is cold, but the people are hospitable."

"You must miss your home."

"I do. But it cannot be my home again until Napoleon and his madmen are stopped."

A movement in the pairs of dancers gave Phoebe time to think about that until the steps reunited her with Mr. Moreau. "Why do they hate magic so much?"

He glanced at Mushroom, who rode Phoebe's shoulder as they danced. "It is unfair, they say, that dragons give an advantage to some but not to others. Your own country fought a civil war over it, did they not? Chopping off King Charles' head when he would not let those without dragons sit in the House of Lords."

"Well, yes, but that was an issue of rights. Some of the dragon-linked even sided against the king. It wasn't a general mania against magic. It's not as though anyone asks to be dragon-linked."

"Do they not? I will be too frank, Miss Hart, and say that your value as a wife is greatly enhanced by the hopes that your bloodline may yet produce others who are dragon-linked."

"Is it an advantage to families, though? Now that any titled gentleman may sit in the House of Lords—and anyone with property can be elected to the House of Commons—it seems to be little more than a novelty."

"Perhaps for the present in England. But the *haut ton* admits you to its ranks not only because it desires your bloodlines, but also so they can keep watch over you, *n'est-ce pas?*"

"Oh. I hadn't considered that. Maybe. But it still seems a bit silly."

"Because you are an innocent. You have not seen how the French dragon-linked sometimes abused their power. Think! There are men and women in this room who can burn with a touch. Who can drown, or lash with whirlwinds, or cause the ground to quake. They don't do so, you are going to protest, but think if they did... and remember that they could."

"That is terrible." Phoebe shuddered. The dance ended, but

she allowed Pierre Moreau to lead her aside. "How does one stop it besides revolution?"

"In England, you are guarded by your peers."

Phoebe nodded. The punishments for using magic to commit a crime were severe. Tried by the members of Parliament who were dragon-linked themselves, the traitors would be hung, drawn, and quartered, as in darker days, and their family forever stripped of the rights to hold office or serve in any government, legal, military, or religious position. It had been enough of a deterrent so far.

Moreau went on. "Many countries have this to some degree —the dragon-linked form a society of some sort to enforce their own rules. Your American colonies are experimenting with governance by a mixture of people and laws that apply to all. But where this does not happen to some degree, you find dictators who can only be overthrown by more powerful dictators."

"Or enough people rising against them," she said quietly.

"*Oui.* Or that. Perhaps it was necessary, but it makes one's home unsupportable."

Phoebe wanted to ask if he had lost anyone in the revolution, but there was no way to do so that would not cause more pain. Before she could finish expressing her sympathy, she sensed someone standing at her elbow.

She turned to find Lord Westing bowing to her, and her heart gave a little jump.

"May I have the next dance?" he asked. His dragon flicked its tongue at Mushroom, who issued a low growl.

"Of course," Phoebe said, too surprised to think of any other answer. She bowed her thanks to Mr. Moreau and let Westing lead her away. So, he was serious about his truce. She couldn't imagine why. He was so far above her, he might be embarrassing himself by stooping to dance with her. Maybe he saw this as penance for his actions at the Queen's Drawing-room. She would not let it discomfit her.

The country dance did not let them stand as close as the waltz had, and Phoebe felt for the first time a twinge of disappointment that Almack's forbade it. She wouldn't allow herself to lapse into stupid silence again, though, so she said the first thing on her mind.

"What do you think of the troubles in France?"

One white-blond eyebrow rose. "I cannot recommend them."

"Of course. But how might we prevent something similar? Are there not also people here who hate the dragon-linked?"

"Mr. Moreau has been pouring his troubles into your ear," he said with such distaste it put her in mind of Hamlet and poisons. "Don't let him fill your head with frightening notions."

"I'm perfectly capable of putting notions in my own head," Phoebe said a little hotly, then she minded her tongue and admitted, "Only now, I don't know how to answer them."

He smiled a little. "You put yourself in a difficult position, then."

"But shouldn't we? Don't we have a responsibility to consider those who might resent us?"

He raised both eyebrows at that. "An interesting thought. We cannot control the actions of others—and especially not what they think of us."

"But we can be responsible for our own actions. Be sure we don't give them reason to hate us."

"Always a wise policy." He added almost to himself, "Make them happy instead."

"I think if they are unhappy, it's because they see unfairness all around them."

"Everything in life is unfair. How would you make it less so, Miss Hart?"

It gave her a pleasant little thrill to hear him say her name, but she quickly put that aside. "Take, for instance, that I am here at Almack's simply because I have a dragon. Does that not give me an unfair social advantage over other ladies whose real accomplishments might make them better suited for it?"

"Disabuse yourself of the notion that it is only having a dragon that admits you into Almack's. I was not on the list until I inherited my father's title," he said sardonically. "But you come from a family of good breeding, you proved yourself to be talented at the Queen's Drawing-room, and—except where stray cats and young boys are concerned—you have... *acceptable* manners."

She looked at him closely. His mouth betrayed no smile, but laughter sparkled in his eyes. He *was* teasing her! "That's no different from dozens of other young ladies."

"Oh, I do not think I could find even half a dozen young ladies like you."

"Very pretty, my lord; I cannot tell if you are complimenting me or insulting me."

"It was a compliment," he said, his voice low.

Phoebe paused, flustered. "Thank you. But it does not answer the imbalance of it all."

"Then I suppose those of us who are dragon-linked must be very aware of our responsibilities. For, as you have said, we have those along with our advantages."

The song came to an end, and Westing bowed. "Thank you for the dance, Miss Hart."

With that, he left. Her heart felt oddly troubled. Just regarding the state of the dragon-linked in England, she told herself.

It did not help when she caught Lady Millicent glaring at her. Despite what Lord Westing said about not being responsible for what others thought of her, she was quite terrified of that lady's baleful expression.

Phoebe arrived home to be told by the butler that a Young Person awaited her in the upstairs sitting-room. She was surprised anyone would be waiting so late at night and wondered if that was the only reason that the butler looked so disapproving. When she hurried upstairs to the sitting-room, she found Deborah entertaining young Jamie. Or, perhaps Jamie was entertaining her, speaking in his heavy street cant while Deborah sparkled with mirth at her efforts to understand him.

"Miss 'Art!" Jamie said.

"Good evening, Jamie. You are out quite late."

Mushroom flapped over to Jamie, and he petted the dragon's head with the delight of a young child. "I don't keep what you'd call regular 'ours, miss. And I 'ad something important to tell you."

Phoebe felt cold at his words. "Oh?"

"I seen that man again, and 'e was lurking about your street."

"Lurking?" Deborah's face went white. "He's found me! I knew he would."

Phoebe put a steady hand on Deborah's shoulder. "Jamie said before that the man was asking about me. We have no reason to fear anyone knows you're here. What was the man doing exactly, Jamie?"

"'E seemed to be just strolling, like, but 'e kept glancing at this 'ouse. I would almost say 'e was casing it, but 'e don't look like a ken cracker."

"Ken cracker?" Deborah asked, her eyes still wide.

"A thief or housebreaker, I believe," Phoebe said.

Jamie nodded. "You've got the right of it, miss. You're a flash mort."

"Well, I don't feel very, er, 'flash.' I don't understand what this man wants with this 'ouse. House. With me. Did you see his face?"

"No, miss. 'E wore a cap pulled down low. I recognize 'is general bearing, if you will, but I can't say for sure about 'is looks."

"Drat. All right. Thank you for coming Jamie." She pulled out a shilling, hesitating when she placed it in his palm. "It's very late. Why don't you curl up downstairs in the kitchen?"

"Really, miss?"

The cook would probably want to skin her for soup the next day, but Phoebe nodded. Jamie's eyes brightened. He likely did not often have a warm place to sleep, and, despite suspicious men lurking on the street, the Jaspers' house was safe. At least, so Phoebe hoped.

Chapter Fifteen

AUNT SERAPHINA WAS DISTRESSED to learn that the strange man had been seen around the house again, but she was determined not to let it ruin Phoebe's social success.

"I believe it may be the work of someone jealous of how well you have taken," she said.

"But Jamie broke into my room before my presentation."

Her aunt wrinkled her forehead at this. "True. Then, someone who dislikes newcomers to the social scene. Either way, we will not let him stop us."

Phoebe doubted her aunt's wisdom in this matter, but her uncle hired an extra manservant specifically to patrol the premises, and Phoebe did not wish to end up locked in the house like Deborah, so she let her aunt guide her.

Her next social engagement was the first of several musicales where she was asked to perform for her peers of the *haut ton*. Her piece was to be last—a grand finale. She wanted to wear her mother's opal bracelet for good luck but didn't dare if it might attract thieves or other criminals.

She sat through the other performances with none of her

usual enjoyment of the music. The back of her neck crawled as if everyone were staring at her. All she could think of was what would happen if she sat at the piano and her magic did not manifest itself. None of her skills on the keys would make up for the audience's disappointment.

"Help me, Mushroom," she whispered to the dragon as she took her place at the piano, but the dragon only stretched on the top of the piano and batted a foreclaw at the candlelight reflecting off the glossy finish.

Phoebe took a deep breath and played a lively toccata, much more cheerful than the piece she had performed at the Queen's Drawing-room. Lights jumped up around her, dancing and swirling in time to the music. A few appreciative whispers rose, but this was nothing like the bright images she had conjured at the drawing-room. Of course, then her emotions had been in a whirl of terror and—yes—anger with Lord Westing for making her feel foolish.

She glanced at the audience. Several of them fidgeted with fans or tugged at watch fobs. Lady Millicent smirked and whispered something to Lady Amelia, who watched with a gleam of pity in her eyes. And there, towards the back, Phoebe spotted a head of white-blond hair. Why did Lord Westing have to be there for her embarrassment?

The balls of light around her burst apart into swarms of glowing bees buzzing to the beat of the music and zipping around the room. Gasps echoed through the audience. A few ladies shrieked and ducked, and Phoebe had to bite her lip to keep from laughing. It was just light. Unlike the more substantial elements, it couldn't hurt anyone.

When the song ended, she received roaring applause, and a rush of people came to congratulate her. She would not tell them, of course, that she hadn't done any of it on purpose. She glanced around for Lord Westing, but Mr. Moreau found her instead, and she could not politely extract herself from his flirtations until her hostess, Mrs. Ashbury, approached her.

"Miss Hart," the lady said, "may I present Mr. Sudbury? He was anxious to make your acquaintance."

A middle-aged gentleman with spectacles and an earnest expression bowed to Phoebe. She curtseyed in return, and Mrs. Ashbury left them, her duty at an end.

"Miss Hart, forgive me for distracting you from your admirers after such a rousing performance."

"You are kind, Mr. Sudbury."

He gave a twitchy smile. "I am a great student of dragon magic, and I have never seen someone use their talent quite as you do."

"Thank you?" Phoebe said, uncertain if he meant it as a compliment.

He stared at Mushroom in fascination. "The gold undertones mean you are attuned to light, but why do you suppose green? Was he always this color?"

Phoebe found it a relief for Mushroom to be the center of attention for once. "I think when he was younger, he might have been a brighter green, with less gold. He's been with me almost as long as I remember, you understand, so I can't perfectly trust my memory."

"Very interesting, but that holds with what I have observed in others. I wonder if he will turn more golden still after you are dead."

Phoebe choked out a surprised chuckle. "I suppose I won't know."

Mr. Sudbury looked back at her, his eyes wide behind his spectacle. "I'm sorry, miss. Forgive my scientific curiosity. I hope you may live a long life."

"As do we all," Westing said from behind her.

She turned. "My lord! We were just discussing the coloration of dragons. May I present to you—"

Westing waved her off. "I am already acquainted with Mr. Sudbury. He is filling in as tutor to my brother while we are in London."

"Oh!" Phoebe turned to Mr. Sudbury. "I suspect Joshua is a clever scholar."

"Tolerably so," Mr. Sudbury said in a distracted tone. "My lord, do you recall the color of your dragon when he was younger?"

Westing looked a little taken aback by this question and glanced at his dragon. "I believe Dragon has always been blue."

"You named your dragon 'Dragon?'" Phoebe asked, her lips twitching in a smile.

"I did," Westing said defiantly. "I seem to recall you called your dragon something a trifle odd."

"Mushroom," Phoebe said, raising her chin, and the dragon looked up at her when she said its name. "Because I found him in the woods. Or, I suppose, he found me. I know now it's a silly name, but I was a child, and it stuck."

"Then we have similar excuses," Westing said with a hint of a smile. "Only I will admit you had more imagination."

Phoebe smiled at him, but Mr. Sudbury went on as if he had not noticed their exchange.

"But the blue is turning paler as time goes by?"

"Er, possibly," Westing said. "And I suppose you're going to tell me he will turn paler still after I die."

Mr. Sudbury nodded. "I suspect so."

The look of suppressed amusement on Westing's face almost made Phoebe lose control of her stifled giggles.

"I have been thinking," Mr. Sudbury went on, "that Joshua would benefit from a visit to the Elgin Marbles at Burlington House."

"Controversial, aren't they?" Phoebe asked. "Because Elgin took them from Greece?"

"That's what makes them educational." Mr. Sudbury glanced

at Mushroom. "I think you would find them edifying for the dragons displayed in them. The human figures are excellent, but to see dragons so much like the ones we know is thrilling."

Westing broke in. "Perhaps Miss Hart would like to accompany us, then." He turned his blue gaze on her. "Joshua would be most gratified to see you again. Of course, you would wish for some escort. Your aunt?"

Phoebe's thoughts raced in confused excitement like a dragon chasing a pearl. "I could talk my brother Max into it. He wouldn't be that interested, but then I would owe him a favor."

They decided they would meet at Burlington House on the following Thursday if it was convenient for Max. Phoebe left the musicale with the distinct sense that it had been a triumph.

"You enjoyed yourself?" Aunt Seraphina asked on the carriage ride home.

"I did."

"I noticed you speaking to Lord Westing."

"Hmm? Oh, yes, I did." Phoebe hesitated, trying to decide how to describe her connection to the man.

"Have a care, dear," her aunt said. "His family is very old, and they are known for being proud. His older brother was expected to marry Lady Millicent, and many people think Lord Westing will do so in his place."

"Of course, aunt," Phoebe said quietly. "You need not fear. I have no expectations of him."

The thought of Lord Westing and Lady Millicent threw dust over all the glow of the night.

Chapter Sixteen

JOSHUA SKIPPED AHEAD of Westing and Sudbury on the stroll to
see the Elgin Marbles.

"Will the dragon lady be there before us?" Joshua asked,
showing where his true interests lay.

"We will find her, either way," Westing said, catching up.
"Unless you run off and I have to take you home."

Joshua looked so abashed that Westing worried he had
spoken too sharply.

"You will especially enjoy the marbles, as your mother is
Greek," Sudbury told the boy, apparently deaf to any reference
to Miss Hart.

Given the unsettled nature of Greece, and his stepmother's
uneasy status as an alien in England, Westing did not want to
draw too much attention to that connection, but Joshua showed
little interest in his heritage.

The great, white marble statues Lord Elgin had stripped
from the Parthenon in Greece now adorned the gardens of
Burlington House. Westing wondered if the partially clad
statues might be a bit much for his young brother but—like Mr.

Sudbury—Joshua was more interested in the dragons than the human figures.

"See this one." Sudbury beckoned Joshua to a statue of a warrior wrestling a dragon. "The Chinese were the first to depict the dragon-linked in their art, but the Greeks may be the most realistic ancient examples. In this case, we do not know if the image represents an actual struggle, perhaps with a wild dragon, or if dragon wrestling was an ancient Greek sport."

Joshua studied the dragon obediently, and Westing took the opportunity to search among the spectators for Miss Hart and her brother.

He found them where the crowds were the thickest, among the triangle of statues taken from the pediment of the Parthenon. Larger-than-life marble gods and goddesses along with their dragon companions loomed over their modern worshippers. Westing stepped past a young man sketching the figures to reach the brother and sister.

Miss Hart's face lit with wonder as she gazed up at the ancient figures, and Westing caught his breath at the sparkle in her eyes.

"How remarkable that stone can look so lifelike!" she said to her brother.

Max held up a quizzing glass and gawked at them. "They don't look lifelike to me. Have you ever seen anyone with muscles like that?"

"Well, I haven't seen quite that *much* of any person except you and our siblings when you were small, and I daresay you did not quite measure up."

Her brother gave her a mock glare. "Besides their musculature, see how many are missing arms and heads and whatnot."

Miss Hart giggled. "When you are a thousand years old, you'll be unlikely to have a head or arms either!

"Touché!" Max said with a bow and a smile. "Just don't go

'round telling the ladies how much your brother resembles these marbles or I won't be able to fend them off."

"Hah!" Miss Hart nudged him with her elbow.

Westing watched them with a stir of jealousy. He would never have been permitted to tease his brother in such a way, and Joshua certainly wouldn't jest with him. He felt that he had missed out on something glowing and cozy.

Miss Hart glanced up and met his gaze. She blushed prettily, and Westing nodded to her, motioning to Sudbury to bring Joshua over.

"Dragon lady!" Joshua called, waving ecstatically.

"Hello, Joshua, isn't it?" She bent just enough to look him in the eye. "Are you enjoying London?"

"Very much, Miss Hart."

"Oh, you know my name. And we haven't been properly introduced."

"My brother told me."

"But I should have introduced you," Westing said. "Miss Hart, my brother, Joshua Langley."

"A pleasure." Miss Hart curtseyed.

"I'm so glad to see you again. You are the kindest lady I know. Not at all fusty like some females."

Miss Hart turned bright pink and laughed. Her dragon, disturbed by her movement, took a flapping leap from her shoulder to perch on the pediment statues next to one of the carved dragons. A few people in the crowd gasped; Westing wasn't sure if they were struck by the likeness or offended that the dragon would dare.

"Your dragon does us a favor," Sudbury said from behind them. "Now we can see how near to reality the sculptors were."

Indeed, though the sculpted dragons had, like the humans, suffered from some missing parts over the years—claws, ridges, and wingtips—they still bore a striking similarity to Mushroom as he perched among the gods and goddesses of the Parthenon.

"He's a bit smaller, though, isn't he?" Max asked. "In comparison, I mean. Artistic license, do you suppose, or were linked dragons larger back then?"

Sudbury nodded. "Good questions! We don't know. Vase paintings from the time show smaller dragons, but of course, dragon bones are unheard of, and even if we found some, we would have no way of knowing if they were from linked or manumitted dragons."

"It hasn't changed much, though, has it?" Miss Hart asked, studying the stone dragons perched near their sculpted companions.

"As far as we can tell, the link between humans and dragons dates back beyond recorded history. Advantageous to both species."

"Is it?" she asked.

"Science still has more questions than answers, but it seems, just as being linked gives humans unusual abilities, it also helps the dragons to draw from their proper elements and grow so that when the human dies, the dragon is strong enough to take its place in the natural order."

Miss Hart nodded.

"It is possible," Sudbury went on, "that dragons are drawn to people who already have a connection with the elements. Some chemical or spiritual property that the dragon can make use of, to the advantage of both."

Miss Hart looked at her dragon in surprise. "I always thought the magic was all on the dragon's side. That we were just their caretakers."

"The magic comes from the dragon," Sudbury said, "but the form it takes may depend on the person it is linked to."

Max nodded. "Phoebs always had a bright personality, even before the dragon showed up. Hardly cried a day in her life, even as a toddler. I remember because all the ones that came after seemed so fussy compared to her."

He beamed at his sister, and she looked away in embarrassed confusion to study the statues again. Westing frowned. If she had attracted a dragon because of her cheerful personality, did that mean he had attracted his because he was naturally cold?

"Do you think," Miss Hart asked quickly, "that the sculptor was dragon-linked?"

Sudbury's eyes widened. "What a clever theory! If he were attuned to earth or stone— perhaps even light—it would make him a more successful artist."

"You mean dragon-linked weren't always kings and all that?" Max asked.

"Not at all!" Sudbury said. "In many cultures, they were more likely to be scholars, healers, or shamans. It was largely in Europe and other aggressive societies that those whose dragons gave them magic used that powers to seize control." At that, Westing caught a look in his eyes that was not altogether friendly.

Miss Hart pinched her lips together. "Yet modern dragon-linked people cannot help if their ancestors were brutal. Most ancestors were, from the histories I've read. And maybe it will change again! With dragon-linked individuals popping up in unexpected lineages, certainly not everyone who is linked will want to take a leadership role. Why, my gown was made by Mrs. Reynolds, who has a dragon but is much more content to be a dressmaker."

"Women may sometimes make such choices," Sudbury said dismissively. "But I wager Lord Westing would say that anyone linked to a dragon has a responsibility to use that power."

Westing eyed him coldly. "You assume too much, Mr. Sudbury. I believe Miss Hart has an interesting point. We have already seen poor leaders who are dragon-linked and wise leaders who are not. I do not believe the mere possession of magic makes someone a fit leader. After all, our king and his dragon are both incapacitated."

"You are a revolutionary," Sudbury said with cackle that made Westing rethink his suitability as a tutor for Joshua.

"I am a realist," Westing said.

"Might they not be the same?" Sudbury asked.

Westing shrugged one shoulder, but Miss Hart gave him a look that he dared hope showed some gratitude or even admiration.

No, he could entertain no such thoughts. Uncle Horace would not approve of Miss Hart. If Westing pursued her, he would lose Joshua, and to a man who would see the boy's innocence as weakness and thrash it out of him. Cold gripped his chest like icy talons.

A gasp rippled through the room, and everyone turned to see a pale-yellow dragon flitting overhead. Miss Hart's mouth opened in a little "o" of wonder, and Sudbury developed a greedy expression.

"The rogue dragon!" he breathed.

The dragon flew overhead as if searching for something. It dove close to Sudbury, and the man flailed to catch it. Westing shook his head. He wouldn't get a dragon that way, no matter how much he wanted it. Then, the rogue dragon perched near Mushroom on the marbles. The two dragons hissed at one another, hopping and circling like wildcats sizing up for a fight, but then the rogue dragon dropped its gaze, and Mushroom bumped heads with it. They chased each other around the marbles, pausing at times to play-fight.

"Extraordinary!" Sudbury said.

This time, Westing agreed with the man. He'd never seen anything like their interaction.

"It won't hurt Mushroom, will it?" Miss Hart asked. "Or lead him away?"

"It doesn't look like it," Westing said. "They seem friendly." He scratched his own dragon's chin. The creature watched its fellows play but did not seem interested in joining them. Hopefully, then, the rogue dragon was no pied piper.

"They seem *very* friendly," Max said. "I don't suppose, I mean, if one were male and one female…"

Sudbury shook off his fascination. "We know little about the reproductive habits of dragons, but they do not seek out a mate so young. They don't even develop distinct gender characteristics until after their human has died. They are rather like very young children at this stage."

The rogue dragon gave Mushroom one last bump of its head and flew off. Mushroom returned to Miss Hart's shoulder, to her obvious relief. The green dragon fluttered its wings in Westing's direction, like a cool acknowledgment of a not-beloved acquaintance and settled down to lick a claw.

"Now, what was that about?" Miss Hart asked her dragon.

"An excellent question," Sudbury said. "I wonder why the rogue has taken such an interest in your dragon."

Miss Hart gave Mushroom a worried look and then glanced at Westing. He wished he could reassure her, but he could not guess what the rogue dragon portended for any of them.

Chapter Seventeen

THE APPEARANCE of the rogue dragon at Burlington House made the papers the next day. Phoebe was grateful to see they had kept her name out of it. Mr. Thayne, dragon advisor to Lord Blackerby, could shed no further light on the dragon's behavior, according to the newspaper account.

Max showed the paper to Deborah, who had heard only a brief account of the day from Phoebe the previous evening.

Deborah's eyes widened as she read, and she went pale. "Do you think the dragon might hurt anyone?"

"It hasn't so far," Phoebe assured her.

"Could... could anyone hurt the dragon, do you think? Or catch it?"

"Mr. Sudbury tried and only looked a fool," Max said with a laugh.

"Mr. Sudbury?" Deborah looked between them.

"A dragon expert," Phoebe said. "But have no fear, I don't think anyone will harm the dragon either. I just wish we knew —" She broke off when she saw Deborah's face. "What is it, dear?"

Deborah held the paper out with a trembling hand. "What is this about?"

It was the notice still running in the personal column, its bold letters appearing every day.

Where there is a dragon there must be a master. Submit peacefully or regret your folly.

"What kind of threat is this?" Deborah asked, her voice trembling. She tossed the paper aside and wrung her hands. "Are we all in danger? I should have known London would be no safer than anywhere else."

"No, dear," Phoebe said. "That ad has been in the paper for some time. I don't think anyone knows what it means, but there has been no specific threat against London."

"Is that not a threat?" Deborah demanded, pointing toward the paper.

"Ravings of a madman," Max said.

Deborah did not look reassured by this. "I think..." She wet her lips. "I thank you for your great kindness, Miss Hart, but I think I must find my aunt soon and beg her to take me away from London."

"We have been searching dear, but we have little to go by. There are thousands of Janets and Janes in London."

"I know." Deborah burst into tears.

"There, there," Max said, patting her hand awkwardly. "If there's anything else you can remember..."

Deborah sniffed and closed her eyes. "My mother took me to see her only once, and I was very small. I remember the streets with their tall houses and so many people."

Phoebe grimaced. That was all of London.

Deborah screwed up her face. "From my aunt's house, we

could see a great building. The largest building I had ever beheld. It had two spires and a dome—such a massive dome as I had never imagined. Dragon gargoyles. And bells. I think it was a church."

Phoebe and Max shared a look and said together, "St Paul's!"

"Is that good?" Deborah asked.

"It gives us an area to search," Phoebe said. "Max can make inquiries for a Janet or Jane in Fleet Street or Cheapside. In the meantime, I'm to go shopping with Aunt Seraphina this afternoon." She smiled at Deborah. "I will find you something pretty to wear when you meet your aunt."

Deborah was all happiness at this scheme, and even Max did not mind being set on a quest, his time at Gentleman Jackson's boxing club, Angelo's fencing academy, the racetracks, and the theater becoming repetitive.

Phoebe set off again for Bond Street with her aunt, more to keep her company than because she needed anything. She found an ostrich feather fan she thought Deborah would like. While she hoped they located the missing aunt, she had grown fond of the exuberant girl.

She was examining the daisies sold by a little girl on the street when Jamie appeared from nowhere, barreling up to her.

"Miss! Miss!"

"Jamie?" She had only seen the boy when he reported to her in Grosvenor Street; he had never approached her in public. "What's wrong?"

"It's terrible, miss! The dragon dressmaker!"

"Mrs. Reynolds?"

"They attacked her. Luddites."

Phoebe dashed after Jamie. She found the bow window of Mrs. Reynolds' shop smashed, shards of glass glinting on the street and a lance jabbed in among the bonnets and silk. The stench of burned fabric hung in the air. A muttering crowd of well-dressed men and women stood around, some half-swooning against their companions. Phoebe's throat tightened as she thought of Mrs. Reynolds' bright smile. Then, she saw the dressmaker standing alone amid the wreckage of her shop.

Phoebe pushed her way through. "Mrs. Reynolds!"

Mrs. Reynolds stared at her, swaying a little on her feet. Black smudges marked her face. "Ah, yes. Light. Pale-yellow silk. Gold spangles."

"What happened here?"

"They attacked the store. I don't understand why. Were they going to rob me? But I didn't let them. I'm attuned to fire." She giggled unsteadily, then grew somber again. "I'm afraid the poor tom cat was singed. He's such a good ratter, I hate to think I did him any harm."

Several Bow Street Runners dashed in to surround Mrs. Reynolds, and Phoebe backed away. Lord Blackerby would have the situation in hand. Phoebe wasn't needed.

The injured tom cat hunched outside the shop, his orange coat patchy with burns and one ear missing a tip. Phoebe approached him, and he tried to limp away, one paw held off the ground. She tossed her shawl over him and bundled him up. The hissing, spitting ball of smoky fur grew still in her arms, no doubt waiting his chance to lash out again.

"We must have you healed," Phoebe told him. "Then you will not be so cross."

Phoebe scanned the crowd for her aunt. She caught dark mutters from the bystanders. Some condemned the Luddites, but others were concerned about Mrs. Reynolds. The fire.

"Not natural. Not safe."

A few shot Phoebe hostile glances.

She shifted the bundled cat, now very conscious of the dragon on her shoulder. Surely, they saw that Mrs. Reynolds had only been defending herself. But the ground was scorched black in front of her shop, and an acrid smell hung in the air.

Phoebe bumped into Lord Blackerby. Grim lines replaced his usual mocking smirk.

"Miss Hart! Did you see what happened?" he asked.

"No. Jamie—Brainy Jamie, that is—might have. He told me about it." She lowered her voice. "This looks bad for the dragon-linked, doesn't it?"

He nodded.

"Did they choose her on purpose?" Phoebe shivered at the realization. "Because her attunement is powerful. And because she is alone. An easier target." She remembered what Mr. Moreau had said about the dragon-linked forming a society. Maybe it wasn't just to police each other.

Blackerby nodded again. "We'd best get you out of sight. I don't like the scent of this crowd. Ah, there's the man for it."

Phoebe looked up and saw Westing descending from his curricle. The crowd parted before him—a man with a dangerous expression and a dragon riding on his shoulder—as he made his way to Blackerby and Phoebe.

"What's all the commotion?" he asked.

"There was an attack," Blackerby said.

"On Mrs. Reynolds," Phoebe put in. "The dragon-linked dressmaker."

"They attacked her now?" Westing asked. "In broad daylight? Why?"

"It appeared to be unprovoked," Blackerby said. "And of course she responded. She's attuned to fire, you see."

"Ah." Westing did see, by the worried look on his face. "Was anyone… hurt?"

"Oh, yes, poor Tom," Phoebe said.

"Tom?" Westing asked. "Who is Tom?"

"The cat." She held up the bundle, which gave a dangerous *mrrrrow.*

A spark of amusement flickered in Westing's eyes, but worry quickly replaced it. "What can I do?" he asked Blackerby.

"First, find Miss Hart's escort—her aunt, I imagine—and take them both home. The streets are too hot, and I want to remove any kindling."

Westing nodded and offered Phoebe an arm. She hesitated, trying to manage the angry cat.

"Here, let me," Westing offered gruffly.

She handed it to him and was glad to accept the steadying strength of his free arm.

"Were any *people* hurt?" he asked.

"Not seriously, I don't think. But they are angry. Some at Mrs. Reynolds, though she was only defending herself."

"What we can do is dangerous," Westing said quietly, with a hint of pain around his eyes.

"Some of... us, I suppose. Do you think we are in danger of revolutionaries here, as in France?"

Westing looked as though he were working that question over, perhaps deciding how much to tell her. His brow drew down. "Perhaps we are."

"I wish being linked were not so... so freakish! I wish anyone who wanted could be linked." Phoebe glanced at Mushroom, who had curled his tail around her neck as though trying to shield her, and she stroked him fondly. "This is too much. If someone attacked me, I have no great element to protect myself."

Westing gave her a warm look. "You are not alone, Miss Hart. No harm will come to you. I will see to it."

She was surprised to find she believed him, and some of her worry drained away, leaving her exhausted.

His grim expression made it easy for them to cut through the curious crowd, and they located Aunt Seraphina craning her neck to see what all the excitement was about.

Phoebe gave her a brief description of the event, and her aunt was quick to accept Westing's offer of an escort home.

When they were safe in his curricle, he handed the cat back into Phoebe's care.

Aunt Seraphina sneezed. "What is that? Something from the fire? It makes my eyes water."

"It's an injured cat," Phoebe said.

"Oh, my dear, they make me itch. You cannot bring that creature to Grosvenor Street."

Phoebe's heart sank. The poor burned cat. And how would Mrs. Reynolds feel to know it had been abandoned? Then she looked at Westing. He stared straight ahead, clearly trying to ignore their conversation, but she gave him a pleading look until he glanced her way with an exasperated quirk of his lips.

Phoebe cradled the growling shawl. "You will take care of him, won't you, my lord? I understand why you wouldn't let Joshua have a cat who didn't need a home, but this poor fellow will require care."

"And you think my brother is suited to the task?"

"He's a good-hearted boy, and it's healthy for young men to have something besides themselves to think about. He will learn responsibility and patience, and the cat will come to like him."

Westing looked dubious, but she could see that he was wavering.

"It would be a great kindness, my lord," she said.

He groaned. "Very well. But the first time it claws Joshua, it will find itself on the street."

"You would not do something so cold-hearted."

And from his grimace, she knew she was right.

After seeing Miss Hart and her aunt safely to Grosvenor Street, Westing sent his groom home with his curricle—and the cat— and returned on foot to Bond Street. The Bow Street Runners had done something to disperse the crowds, but Blackerby was still questioning witnesses.

Mrs. Reynolds sat in the empty frame of her bow window, her dragon curled up on her lap. She sipped tea and stared blankly at the spot where she had scorched the ground. She noticed Westing watching her, and her eyes flitted to his dragon.

"I've caused some trouble, haven't I?" she asked. She did not sound entirely repentant of it.

"I'd say whoever attacked you caused the trouble."

She swirled the tea in her cup, watching the brown liquid go around. "I don't often use my element. It's not much use to a dress maker. Fabric and fire make an unfortunate combination."

Westing nodded. "It's not always useful to us." He studied her rather dazed expression and said in a low voice, "It can be frightening, being dangerous."

She smiled a little. "I only want to be dangerously fashionable. I don't know why they can't leave me alone. I didn't even try to assert myself higher."

"I don't think hate and fear are rational," Westing said. "But hopefully soon you can settle back down to business."

She nodded, but her gaze rested again on the scorched stones in front of her shop.

Blackerby noticed Westing and his eyebrows went up.

He gestured Westing over. "Return to gawk at the destruction? Behold, the wages of our wickedness!"

"It is becoming dangerous, isn't it?" Westing asked.

"Becoming? My dear boy, when the first heads rolled in France, that's when it started 'becoming.'"

"At any rate, I see I cannot ignore it. At some point, it will harm someone I care about."

Blackerby's face lit up. "Do you mean to help us, then?"

"I mean, I'm in it whether I like it or not."

"Fabulous. I love a reluctant volunteer." Blackerby grinned

gleefully and strode off to disperse a group of boys trying to steal charred souvenirs from in front of the shop.

"I'm glad you'll be 'elping," Jamie said from behind.

"I thought you worked for Miss Hart," Westing said. "Have you been spying on her for Blackerby?"

His eyes widened. "Never, sir. I'm loyal to my mistress. I keep all of 'er secrets," he said in a way that made Westing wonder what secrets she could be keeping. "But if the shadow lord can 'elp 'er, then I'll do what I can to 'elp 'im, too. And that's why I like you—you care about 'er"

"I wish to be of service to her, at least."

At some point, she would probably want help finding employment for Jamie. He might make an excellent Bow Street Runner, but Westing began to wonder if a clever lad should have other options as well. He would have to ask around about possibilities for educating the boy.

As he wandered home, his thoughts about young Jamie's future blended into worries about his own. He wasn't entirely sure what he had committed himself to when he offered to help Blackerby, but he would not see his family hurt by Luddites or revolutionaries.

He was disturbed to find that, in his imaginings of the days ahead, Miss Hart made frequent appearances. She was not the kind of girl his father or uncle would approve of—too likely to do something unconventional and set everything on its ear. Like saddling him with an injured cat. His father would hate the idea of that creature passing the threshold of their townhouse. But when Westing thought of Miss Hart's pleading eyes, he accepted that his fate and the cat's were destined to go together for a time.

Chapter Eighteen

SHORTLY AFTER BREAKFAST the next morning, Phoebe withdrew to
the library, seeking a distraction from the previous day's events.
The newspapers blamed it on thieves, but Phoebe suspected
Lord Blackerby had manipulated the story. Her aunt had the
latest Miss Charity book, and Phoebe decided gleaning bits of
gossip from its caricatures was as good a way to occupy her
mind as any. She turned the pages with a guilty thrill,
recognizing many of the figures she knew from balls and
musicales in their translated form in Prince Arthur's court.

A newly introduced lady sleep-walked through the court
with a glowing ball cupped in her hands. Phoebe gasped and
leaned forward. Was this her? The physical description was a
flattering caricature of herself, even down to the details of her
court gown. She had made Miss Charity's pages! But why did
Miss Charity depict her as a sleepwalker?

As Phoebe puzzled over the book, the butler announced
himself by clearing his throat. His face, once again, looked
disapproving, and she wondered if Jamie had returned. But the

butler offered his tray with a card bearing the name of the Earl of Blackerby.

"To see me?" Phoebe asked uncertainly.

"That is what the gentleman requests, miss."

"Very well." She considered that. The earl was not courting her, so he probably wished to speak about the previous day. So much for her distraction. "Ask my aunt to come to me and see him in."

Phoebe set her book aside and straightened her gown. Ribbons of darkness swirled around the threshold of the library. The young footman by the door stiffened, his eyes wide.

The butler shot the footman a warning look and announced, "His Lordship, the Earl of Blackerby."

Blackerby paused to study the footman like a specimen in a butterfly case. The footman didn't twitch, but he stood so straight he looked like he might fall over backward, and a trickle of sweat appeared at his hairline. Blackerby smiled with angelic innocence and turned to Phoebe.

"If you insist on having a chaperone, ask for your uncle or aunt instead of this poor fellow. They should also know what I have to tell you. Oh, but Lord Jasper is unlikely to be at home, am I correct?"

Blackerby said this with a smirk, but Phoebe ignored the jab at her uncle's domestic failings. "I have already sent for Aunt Seraphina." She motioned for the footman to leave, and he hurried out, his eyes wide with relief.

Blackerby's dark gray dragon stalked forward, and Mushroom jumped up to intercept it. The two dragons circled each other, then Blackerby's dragon snorted and trotted over to curl up in the shade beneath the sofa. Mushroom hopped up to bask on the windowsill.

Blackerby glanced down at the book Phoebe had set aside. "You are enjoying Miss Charity's tales?"

"They are very diverting, and... well, I admit I am pleased to see a likeness of myself in this one."

He smiled. "But one is not supposed to confess to recognizing oneself in Miss Charity's books, for if you see yourself—and I admit Miss Charity has painted a pretty picture of you—others will have to see themselves as well and may not be so flattered."

"Oh," she said uncertainly.

"No need to trouble yourself over me," Blackerby said. "My vanity is not such that being the court jester insults me. Besides, I think Miss Charity may be rather fond of me, for the jester is wise, is he not?"

"He is," Phoebe said, though she also thought the jester was a sad, lonely figure.

"I suppose you have no trouble recognizing some of your friends as well. The stone knight?"

Phoebe flushed. "Perhaps."

"Yes, perhaps. Ah, Lady Jasper, I'm glad you could join us."

Aunt Seraphina gave the earl a wary look. "I came as soon as I could. It sounds as if you have something momentous to say."

"I do. I understand, Miss Hart, that your young spy has seen your watcher again."

Phoebe gave a start. "I... How did you know?"

He smiled. "It is my business... nay, my duty to know. Have no fear, though. It was not your young friend who alerted me."

"Very well," Phoebe said. "He did warn me recently that the man had returned."

"He's a useful lad. You were clever to recruit him. It's too bad that I cannot call on a lady to become one of my under-secretaries."

"Thank you?"

"Indeed. But I think we need more information than the lad can provide."

"What do you mean, my lord?" Aunt Seraphina asked.

"As Secretary of the Home Department, I need to know if there might be spies or insurrectionists in our midst."

"You don't suspect my niece of being a spy?"

Blackerby gave Phoebe an amused glance. "Not much. But between the attack on Mrs. Reynolds yesterday and this unknown man watching your house, I feel uneasy."

"His attentions could be romantic. Twisted infatuation," Aunt Seraphina said.

"In my experience, those with such deranged affections don't content themselves with only watching. They might leave gifts. Something that would seem disturbing to the well-ordered mind. Or try to steal things of the lady's. Has any such thing occurred?"

Phoebe shook her head, repressing a shudder.

"In that case, I must look more deeply into this."

"I'm not... I'm not important enough for such attention," Phoebe said.

"You are dragon-linked, Miss Hart. And, you are a dragon-linked from a family not previously known for such a trait. This phenomenon is upsetting to some."

"Are you suggesting the Luddites are threatening Phoebe?" Aunt Seraphina asked.

"I fear the possibility."

Phoebe dug her fingers into the velvet sofa. "Why? I haven't done anything."

"Unfortunately, there are zealots among their number, and zealots rarely care for what is reasonable."

"Must I leave London?" Phoebe asked.

"Heavens, no! Nothing could be more dangerous than move to somewhere more remote. Here, at least, you are under the eyes of many guardians. I might..." he trailed off, looking thoughtful. "I might have a Bow Street Runner come to work at your home, Lady Jasper. It must not be common knowledge. He could..."

"He could spy," Aunt Seraphina said disdainfully.

"Exactly. Oh, not on you, of course." He flashed a mocking grin. "Just on those coming and going."

Aunt Seraphina stared at the cold fireplace. Phoebe bit her lip and looked down at her hands folded demurely in her lap. She did not like the idea of a Bow Street Runner shadowing her every move, but she was more frightened that a fanatic might hate her. For what? Something she was born with and had no control over.

"Very well," Aunt Seraphina said. "Provided my husband does not object, I will allow one of your runners to come in as a groom."

"A groom?" Blackerby said.

Her eyebrows shot up. "Do you have a runner who would look anything but ridiculous as a footman?"

Blackerby laughed at that. "No, madam. I admit they are not a handsome lot."

"And I assume some of them might know their way around horses? Well enough to pass, at least. A groom could accompany my niece when she goes out just as easily as a footman could."

Blackerby's eyes brightened. "Quite right. And I know just the man."

"Should I go anywhere, though?" Phoebe grimaced. "We could let it be known that I have… measles. Until we catch this man—"

"You would be willing to hide away?" Blackerby asked. "You did not strike me as the shrinking type."

"I'm not, I don't think. But I don't court trouble, either."

"You may restrict your activities if you like." Aunt Seraphina looked disappointed at that, but Blackerby went on, "Don't stop all your social engagements, however. With my man at your back, we may lure the enemy into the open."

"Serve as bait!" Phoebe said.

"Instead, think of it as acting the part of a spy."

Aunt Seraphina curled her lip in disgust, but Phoebe met Blackerby's expectant gaze. Spies—and actors—were not considered reputable, and female spies must be a thousand times worse. But Phoebe was in a position to help her country. To help Mrs. Reynolds and everyone else before the Luddite troubles came to bloodshed. No one had to know she was assisting Lord Blackerby, and it seemed—if not proper, at least morally justified.

She nodded. "I'll do it."

Chapter Nineteen

WESTING RETURNED from his afternoon drive with Joshua to be accosted by his valet, Jenkins. The long-faced man held out one of Westing's black coats as if it had been dredged from a sewer.

"Jenkins?"

"My lord." Jenkins voice cracked. "There are animal hairs on this coat."

Westing raised his quizzing glass. "So there are. They appear to be Tom's."

"This is a Stultz." Jenkins said. He shook the coat, but gently. "A Stultz!"

"Surely, such a work of art cannot be ruined by a few cat hairs."

Jenkins face drooped. "I have served you faithfully, have I not, my lord?"

"And I hope you will continue to do so for many years." Westing patted the valet on the shoulder and scooted past him. Perhaps it was time to increase Jenkins' pay.

In the front hall, a letter from Uncle Horace waited on the mail tray. Westing scowled and tore it open. He'd kept Sudbury

on despite his odd comments at Burlington House to satisfy his
uncle's demand that Joshua have a tutor. What else did Horrible
Horace want?

His face darkened as he read.

*Word has reached me that you are consorting with a woman whose
status is not equal to your own. I will not see our family name lowered
or dragged through sordid gossip. If you cannot make wise decisions
for yourself, I cannot trust you to make wise decisions for Joshua. I will
be forced to remove him from your care.*

Ice rippled over the letter, smudging the words. Westing wished
he was attuned to fire so he could turn the paper to ash. Instead,
he tore it and wadded the pieces for Dragon to attack.

So, it was to be Phoebe Hart or his brother? Westing rubbed
his crooked nose. There was no legal way to overturn his
father's will. Even his stepmother couldn't do anything to free
Joshua from Horace, especially since she was foreign.

Joshua dashed down the corridor. "West, sir, you should see
how well Tom is doing. His burns are scabbing up nicely, and
he's drinking loads of cream from his saucer."

"I imagine he is," Westing said, trying to smile. "I hope he
repays us by catching many fat rats."

"Of course, he will!" Joshua skipped away.

Pain burned in Westing's chest, a searing tear through his
core. Horace could never get his hands on the boy. Westing had
to obey.

He retreated to his study and drew off his gloves. Dragon
hissed a warning. A movement in the corner of Westing's eye
made him jump, and he turned to see Blackerby sitting with his
feet propped on a low table and a book in his lap. Shadows
settled around him.

"What the devil!" Westing advanced on the man. No matter his position in the government, he could not go around sneaking into people's homes. Westing would knock sense into him if he had to.

"Not the devil, my friend." Blackerby grinned. "Do you enjoy Miss Charity's books?"

The non-sequitur stopped Westing mid-stride. "What?"

"Miss Charity's novels. Knights of the Round Table."

"I have not read them."

"Oh, dear! Poor Miss Charity putting all this effort into her work, giving you an interesting role and everything, and you simply ignore it."

"A role in her book? You don't mean she's written about me?" Westing was appalled. He did not want to be made a public figure. He didn't know why he should be.

"Not enough that you could sue the publisher for libel, but everyone else must see the resemblance."

Westing glowered at that. "Let everyone else do what they like. Think what they like. I assume you didn't break into my house to talk about literature."

"I didn't break in at all. Your poor cook let me in. Didn't quite know what else to do when an earl came knocking at the servants' entrance. But your butler kept saying you weren't at home. I thought, perhaps, you just weren't at home to me, and it wounded me."

Westing rolled his eyes. "What do you want?"

"I want your eyes and ears, Westing. They are sharp. There are dangers about, and I can only see them through a glass, darkly." He gestured at the shadows coiling about his feet. "You received an invitation to a party hosted by Monsieur Pierre Moreau."

"You know my mail better than I do, I suppose. What about it?"

"He's a charming young man. An admirer of Miss Hart."

That irritated Westing, but he would not show it. "And?"

"I would like you to attend his gathering. Firstly, because Miss Hart will be there, and I'm concerned for her safety with the Luddites stirring."

"Then encourage her to stay home."

Blackerby raised a finger. "That brings me to my second reason. I want Miss Hart to go to this event. I hear rumors. Follow undercurrents. Moreau or his associates may have Luddite or revolutionary sympathies, and Miss Hart could ferret them out."

"Unacceptable," Westing said.

"*You* are not in a position to decide what Miss Hart does, and she has already agreed. I am sending a Bow Street Runner, Farris, to watch her, but he cannot mingle the way you can."

This would not do. Westing had to stay away from Miss Hart. He wished he could take Blackerby into the boxing ring and draw his cork, but the earl was not a sportsman. Instead, Westing spoke through gritted teeth. "Very well."

"Excellent! I knew you could be reasonable. I'll leave Miss Charity's book for you."

"You may as well not."

Blackerby smiled sweetly and strode away from the book. "Good evening, Lord Westing."

Westing rolled his eyes at Blackerby's back, but his gaze drifted to the book, and he ran his fingers over the smooth, waxed leather cover. No, he didn't care what others said about him. He left it and went to bed.

When he came down to breakfast in the morning, he was surprised to find Joshua already at the table, leaning hungrily over Miss Charity's book. Westing felt a pang of misgiving. Some novels were too sensational for children, male or female. Uncle Horace would forbid such books. Dragon glided over to sit on Joshua's shoulder and stare at the book as though he were reading it, too.

"What do you have there?" Westing asked.

"Oh, it's fantastic! Full of knights fighting monsters. It's not the sort of King Arthur story I've heard before. There's no Lancelot, and more ladies than I remember. Some even go into battle. I don't understand all the characters, though."

"Oh?" Westing asked, dishing some ham from the sideboard.

"Yes. There's this stone knight. He's really strong and brave. He reminds me of you. He even has white hair. But sometimes he just watches while bad things happen."

Westing's hand froze over the boiled eggs. "He does?"

"Yes. I suppose it's because of the wizard's curse turning him to stone. A person made of stone wouldn't be able to move very fast. The magic has almost reached his heart. I hope it doesn't kill him."

Westing sat at the table with his ham, his appetite gone. Was this what Blackerby meant when he said they were writing about him? He had been made into some sort of heartless creature?

Joshua chattered on about Tom's recovery, oblivious to his brother's glowering mood, for which Westing was grateful. He was not heartless. It was ridiculous for this Miss Charity, whomever she—or he?—was, to make such assumptions about him. The author didn't even know him.

Because he never gave anyone a chance to, a little voice in his mind scolded him. For the best. If they did know him, they would have more opportunities to be disappointed. His father had taught him that. Keep people at a distance, and he could keep his spotless image intact. Like a stone statue of family pride.

After breakfast, he sent Joshua to his studies and took Miss Charity's book for himself. The more he read, the deeper the leaden feeling sunk into his stomach. He recognized many of the characters in the book. And the caricatures were accurate, or seemed to be. Did that mean this author had dissected him correctly as well? Or did it mean, like Miss Charity, that he was looking too much on the surface of people and not seeing them fairly?

Blackerby's character interested him. The court jester. Yes, Blackerby probably enjoyed that. The wise fool. Always playing some sleight-of-hand game. Perhaps Blackerby was the author. It seemed fitting. A way to share his mockery with the widest possible audience. And of course, he would enjoy laughing at everyone as they laughed at each other.

Westing put the book aside and paced in his study, the image of the stone knight worrying him more than it should have. Dragon flapped up to his shoulder, and Westing rested a hand on his companion's warm scales. He liked to think of himself as a protector, standing aloof from the troubles around him. But did that mean he was being too cold? He thought of Miss Hart. Uncle Horace forced him to be cold. Was that his wizard?

He stopped to frown at the family seal. Duty first. He moved it to its old place and then back to where it was more convenient for him.

At least he would go to Mr. Moreau's party and be certain that Miss Hart stayed safe.

Chapter Twenty

"I SEE NO OTHER CHOICE," Phoebe told Max and Deborah in the sitting room. "Max can't narrow it down enough to find your aunt, so we will have to go looking for her."

"If I leave, *he* may find me," Deborah said, her eyes wide.

Phoebe patted her hand. "If you stay here, Blackerby's man is likely to see you. And we may be in danger from the man stalking this house. I suspect your aunt is in Cheapside, and if we take you there, it might stir your memories. You could be out of the frying pan."

"Into the fire?" Deborah asked, her voice trembling. "Oh, but the frying pan is very frightening, too."

"I'm hoping *not* into the fire," Phoebe said. "You do wish to find refuge with your aunt?"

Deborah turned anguished eyes to her and then to Max. "I do. Very well. I will throw my fate to the winds of chance and seek my aunt."

"You'll come with us, won't you Max?" Phoebe asked.

"Only too glad, though you'll be looking for a needle in a haystack." He grinned. "Or a Haymarket."

Phoebe rolled her eyes. "No, Cheapside."

"As long as you promise not to do any shopping. I'm not carrying your hatboxes!"

"Of course not."

Inspired by her aunt's early idea, Phoebe wrapped Deborah in a black veil so that, if she did not look like a Spanish lady, she at least looked like she was in mourning and hiding from public view. Phoebe found Jamie haunting the kitchen and sent him out to check that their path was clear, and after he assured her it was, Phoebe and Deborah went out to wait for Max in the Jasper's carriage.

"Leave it to a man to keep us waiting," Phoebe said, peering out the window. "He didn't use to care so much for his cravat. It's London, I suppose."

"He does tie it so elegantly," Deborah said.

Phoebe chuckled. It was hard to think of her brother as elegant when she had seen him dunked in the fishpond and tumbled from his pony as a child.

Something fluttered against the window.

"What on earth?" Phoebe asked, craning to look out. "Did a bird just hit us?"

Deborah shrank back.

The thing slammed into the carriage, tearing a hole in the fabric roof. Phoebe's heart gave a start, and Deborah quailed against her.

A pale-yellow reptilian head poked into the carriage and hissed at them.

"The rogue dragon!" Phoebe said.

Mushroom flared his wings and hopped about but made no move to attack.

The other dragon tore at the carriage again, opening a rift wide enough for its body to fit through. Phoebe moved to shield Deborah.

"It's not a rogue dragon," Deborah said quietly.

"What?" Phoebe asked.

"It's mine."

Phoebe gaped at Deborah, who held out her hand to the pale-yellow dragon.

"Rahab," Deborah called.

The dragon hopped over and rubbed its head against her chin.

"You're linked!" Phoebe said.

Deborah nodded, looking like she was going to cry, though she was stroking the dragon's head fondly.

"But—but I thought you were afraid of dragons!"

"Only afraid of what they can do. What they can make me do."

"What are you attuned to?"

Deborah looked down and swallowed hard.

"Deborah?"

"Lightning. I'm attuned to lightning. It is the most terrible thing." A tear hung on her lashes for a moment then rolled down her cheek.

Phoebe considered the implications. "That could be frightening. We should find someone who might be able to help you—"

"No!" Deborah said violently. "No one can know. Don't you understand how dangerous I am?"

She burst into sobs.

"Quick, back in the house." Phoebe grabbed Deborah's veiled form, throwing her cloak over her to hide the dragon she cradled, and ushered her inside.

"Max!" she called, rushing Deborah to the sanctuary of the sitting room.

"What happened?" He jogged in, his cravat still akimbo. He saw the dragon sitting on Deborah's lap and stopped, eyes wide. "She's dragon-linked! I didn't think it could happen so late in life. Not that Miss Sloan is old, of course."

Deborah sniffled and buried her face in a handkerchief.

"She is not newly linked," Phoebe said. "She was hiding from her dragon—the rogue dragon."

"Why?" Max asked.

Deborah sniffed again but managed to get her voice under control. "I don't want to be attuned. Rahab is a sweet little thing, but I don't want to be dangerous."

"She's attuned to lightning," Phoebe said softly, in response to Max's confused look.

His eyes widened again. "That's extraordinary! What an exciting thing—" he caught Phoebe's subtle headshake and stopped himself. "I mean, so sorry you're dealing with something so frightening, Miss Sloan. Bet you could learn to control it." He cocked his head in thought for a moment. "Perhaps not right here, in London—"

But Deborah was shaking her head. "You don't understand. It's not just Rahab I was hiding from. It's... people want me to use my abilities to... to hurt other people. I don't want to do it."

But she could, Phoebe realized. Not many attunements were as dangerous as lightning. Fire, maybe. This was why society kept tabs on the dragon-linked. Society had missed Deborah, but someone else had not.

"Who are you hiding from, Deborah?" Phoebe asked. "Could they know you are here?"

Deborah's eyes flew open. "Oh, I have put you in danger, have I not? I should have just stayed in that ditch and died!" She began bawling again.

"Now, there!" Max said, alarmed. "None of that! We're glad you didn't die in that ditch. We will protect you."

"Indeed." Phoebe soothed Deborah's back. "But we cannot help you if you don't tell us a little more about who we're protecting you from."

Deborah's sobbing slowed and she took a deep breath. "It's the Luddites. My family were members."

"And they had a child who was dragon linked?" Phoebe asked softly. What a terrible thing.

Deborah nodded. "They tried everything to break the link, but they couldn't. Couldn't kill the dragon. And it hurt me when they attempted it."

Max's mouth pressed into a thin line.

"Finally, they decided God had delivered me into their hands to use as a weapon against the dragon-linked. I would infiltrate Society and hurt them." Her voice dropped to a whisper. "They wanted me to strike at the Queen's Drawing-room."

Max and Phoebe sat in shocked silence. Phoebe thought of the huge crowd there: the queen, the prince and the dukes, so many members of Parliament. A lightning storm among them. The smell of burned cat fur from Mrs. Reynold's shop returned to her, and she held in a gag.

"If God delivered the Luddites into my hands—" Max began, but Phoebe cut him off with a shake of her head. She agreed with the sentiments, but Deborah was in a fragile state. It was not the time.

"The first part of their plan has failed," Phoebe said. "You did not attend the Queen's Drawing-room, and we are aware of that danger now. They may not know you are here, though Brainy Jamie's watching man worries me. What protection did you hope for from your aunt?"

"My mother's family did not agree with the Luddites. I think she would understand the danger and hide me."

"You still may be safer here. The Luddites would not dare attack the house of a lord in the center of London."

"You do not know what they would dare," Deborah said. "They can never find out I am here. They have spies everywhere, even among the *haut ton*."

"Do you know who?" Phoebe asked, her mind racing to Lord Blackerby. He was Secretary of the Home Office, responsible for keeping England safe. He would make good use of that knowledge.

But Deborah shook her head. "They never told me. I was just a tool to them, especially once my parents died. I have always suspected... it's terrible to say, but my uncle was much crueler than them, and I have wondered if their deaths weren't an accident. To him, I was useful but never trusted. Never loved. He said I was an abomination. And I'm so afraid he will find me."

"Never," Phoebe said. "We'll keep you inside. Your dragon, too. We won't let anyone know you're here. At least not until we know who we can trust. Lord Blackerby might—"

"No, please! I don't know who I should trust, but I trust you. Please, don't tell anyone about me yet. You promised you would keep me hidden, and my uncle could be anywhere."

"What is his name?" Max asked at the same time Phoebe said, "What does he look like?"

"He would not use his real name, and he is an expert at disguising himself. I don't know what he might look like now. A footman, a nobleman, even a woman."

Phoebe considered that. Deborah had information about the Luddites' plans, but not about a specific threat anymore. Keeping her hidden a bit longer probably wouldn't hurt anyone, and if the girl's uncle was so adept at blending in, the best thing to do would be to help Lord Blackerby ferret out the Luddites. She would warn Jamie to be extra alert for the lurking stranger.

"We will keep your secret," Phoebe said. "Unless someone's life is in danger because of it."

Deborah bit her lip and nodded. She stroked her dragon's back as it circled and jumped around her, as happy as a puppy to be reunited. No wonder it had been drawn to Mushroom; it probably smelled its mistress. People would wonder at the sudden disappearance of the rogue dragon, but the Luddites were a much bigger concern.

Chapter Twenty-One

BLACKERBY'S MAN arrived in the form of Mr. Farris, a red-headed man whose strapping size would look more at home on the docks than in a drawing-room.

"He never could have been a footman," Aunt Seraphina said, shaking her head.

"He can probably pick the horses up if he needs to clean under them," Phoebe added with a chuckle.

Farris was friendly enough, though he mostly stayed out of the way. Nevertheless, Phoebe let it be known that her friend Miss Sloan was ill to be sure the servants stayed away and did not see Rahab. They could not have that bit of gossip leaking out.

Farris's first real opportunity to prove his usefulness as a guard would be Phoebe's attendance at Mr. Moreau's party. Lord Blackerby wanted her to listen for revolutionary gossip. She still felt duplicitous, but she didn't want to see another attack like at Mrs. Reynold's shop.

Deborah joined Phoebe as she tried to select the dress she would wear. She held up a white muslin stitched with pink flowers—one of the dresses she had brought from home. It did not match Mushroom, though, so it was not right for London. She sighed and selected the yellow gown with green sprigging instead. That would do better. Would Lord Westing like it? She shouldn't concern herself with that. He was destined for the likes of Lady Millicent.

Deborah eyed the dresses enviously. "Oh, I wish I could go with you! I'm so afraid I will never attend a party or a ball!"

Phoebe sat beside her. "I'm sure you will. We will not have to keep you in hiding forever. The people looking for you will eventually give up or... or die of old age."

"But probably not until I am much too old to enjoy myself."

Phoebe managed not to laugh at the poor girl. The only way out of her troubles was to uncover the Luddites, and this party might be their opportunity.

Max drove Phoebe to Pierre Moreau's temporary home on Park Street. Judging by the size of the townhouse, Moreau was more comfortable than most refugees from the French troubles.

Farris's presence in the groom's seat behind them reminded her that this was not a mere pleasure excursion. Max's eyes were bright with the adventure of acting as a spy, and though Phoebe hoped it would be a sedate event, she squirmed in her seat.

A group of men gathered on the street opposite the townhouse. They wore the rough clothes of laborers and several had scarred faces that suggested they lived hardscrabble lives. They weren't doing anything—just standing around with their hands shoved in their pockets—but the way they glowered at the party guests gave Phoebe a crawling sense of unease.

Farris had to part ways with Phoebe and Max at the front door, and they found the party already a crush. Noisy groups played faro and roulette, and the musicians performed waltzes that couples enjoyed in a dimly lit garden. Phoebe and Max shared a wary look. This was not quite as respectable a party as they had been led to believe.

"The French!" Max whispered with a shudder. "Where do you suppose we hear anything interesting?"

"No doubt where people are drinking the most."

"The gardens, then."

They squeezed their way outside where, indeed, footmen carried trays laden with glasses of wine and ratafia for the guests. Other footmen held torches aloft to illuminate the dancing couples.

A group of giggling ladies spotted Phoebe. One whispered to another, and Phoebe caught the name "Westing." The ladies fell into a fresh round of raucous laughter. One of them lost her balance and sat on the edge of a fountain with a splash. Her companions shrieked in merriment.

Phoebe shut her eyes and took a deep breath of air that smelled of wine and smoke and sweat. Something in her chest fluttered at hearing herself linked with Lord Westing, but it died with the idea that she was making a laughingstock of them both. Especially herself.

Blackerby had made a mistake in sending her. Perhaps he had just been using them to sneak Farris into the party. Hopefully, the grooms were drinking as copiously as the guests and had loose tongues.

Mr. Moreau approached Phoebe, his steps a little unsteady. He performed an elaborate bow, and she was surprised he didn't tip over.

"Misss H-hart," he slurred. "I did not have the pleasure of waltzing with you in the past. Surely you will not refuse me now and break my heart?"

Max shifted, and he looked like he would be happy to break *something* of Moreau's, but Phoebe put a hand on his arm. Moreau seemed too young to be Deborah's uncle, but he did talk like a Luddite at times. He might know something. She allowed him to guide her to the center of the gardens to dance. Fortunately, he only stepped on her foot once, and he did not hold her too close as she had feared. Unfortunately, he had drunk enough that his conversation was not enlightening, unless Phoebe wished to know his views of the English opera or the horse race where he lost a great deal of money.

"And they promised me this jockey only came in first! Bah! Oh, but the dance is at an end. Thank you, Miss Hart, for your charming company. I hope I may call on you sometime soon?"

Phoebe made a noncommittal reply and escaped Moreau. If clues about the Luddites had been buried in his gregarious ramblings, she was not clever enough to dig them out. And now, she had lost Max. They were supposed to stay together, but they had not counted on how chaotic the party would be.

"Miss Hart!" Eliza motioned her over.

Phoebe hurried to her side, grateful to see a friendly face. But Deborah's warning flitted through her mind. Her uncle could appear in many guises. Eliza was tall, of rather heroic proportions for a woman. But, no, Phoebe could not believe she was a Luddite in disguise. Besides, she was dragon-linked. That couldn't be faked.

Captain Parry lingered nearby. Phoebe knew little of him, though he was often present in the background. Watching.

"Dancing with our host?" Eliza asked.

"Yes, though he's already had too much to drink."

Eliza laughed. "I'm not surprised. He was drinking like a lord earlier this evening, and I don't think he's let up. It feels good in the garden, though, does it not? Inside, it's so sticky I feel like I'm in Dominica again."

"It is very hot there, I suppose?"

Eliza's eyes sparkled with humor. "Very. We even have a lake of boiling water. People suspect a fire dragon sleeps at the bottom of it, though why he would be underwater, no one knows."

"Do you miss it there?"

"Sometimes. But this is a new adventure, so I don't look

back."

"Did you know Captain Parry in the West Indies? It seems you've been acquainted with each other for some time."

"I did. I cannot escape the man." She lowered her voice. "I will admit, he's often useful for driving off unwanted attention. I don't trust a thing any of these men say, and I find it tiring to be always on guard. If only we could disguise ourselves as men and spy on them, then we would know whom we could trust."

Phoebe laughed. "I suppose I must leave it to my brother to do my spying for me. Captain Parry often warns you of ill-intentioned men, then?"

Eliza rolled her eyes. "He says they're all ill-intentioned. I hope for the sake of humanity that is not true."

Phoebe glanced at Captain Parry, who was watching over them not-too-subtly.

"Miss Prescott!" called Lord Blanchfield. "You promised me a dance tonight. You have put me off long enough."

"Speaking of ill-intentioned!" Eliza whispered to Phoebe. "But, then, he is an earl's eldest son, and it would be amusing to be a countess someday."

Eliza went off with Lord Blanchfield, and Phoebe risked a glance at Captain Parry, who watched them with a troubled frown. Eliza was only teasing, though. She wouldn't marry a man just for his title. At least, Phoebe hoped she would not.

If Eliza had known Captain Parry that long, though, he was not Deborah's uncle, and probably not a Luddite, either.

Lady Millicent stood nearby, sourly watching her brother dance with Eliza. Lady Amelia fanned herself and scanned the crowds with a little curl of amusement to her lips. She caught Phoebe's eye and gave her a friendly nod.

Left without an escort, Phoebe made her way to a table where she could fetch a glass of ratafia and so not look as awkward. She sat and sipped it, realizing that holding still had its benefits. Moreau's guests wandered past, bringing snatches of conversation with them. She was glad her mother had insisted they learn a little French, but in this case, it only let her discover more than she wished about the love lives of some of the *haut ton.*

Lady Millicent strolled by, whispering to Lady Amelia. "A dog is one thing, I suppose, but keeping a cat? An ugly, mean-spirited one, too, from what I've heard. Half the town thinks he's gone mad."

Lady Amelia raised her coppery-red eyebrows. "Perhaps the house has mice."

"Oh, really, Amelia. It's dear of you to try to make the best of it, but what a disgusting thought." Mushroom gave a low growl at the lady's dragon, and Millicent glanced Phoebe's way. "None of his true friends would want to see him so humiliated."

She snapped open her fan and walked on. Lady Amelia paused to glance at Phoebe and mouthed the word, "Harpy."

Phoebe chuckled a little, wondering why Lady Amelia associated with Lady Millicent. It was expected of them, she supposed. And it might be expected of Phoebe to stop putting Lord Westing in situations that lowered his public standing. She wasn't trying to harm his reputation. She just didn't understand all the proprieties. The rules of his world. Dragon or no, it was not where she belonged. She tried to do right but only embarrassed herself at every turn.

The thought put her into a blue study, and she stared absently at the dancing couples in the garden. But then the word "dragon" caught her ear—in English, not French. Two young men, deep in serious conversation. Phoebe pretended to take no notice of them and looked for Max, but he was still nowhere to be seen. Drat! The men were returning to the house. She set her ratafia aside and strolled after them as nonchalantly as possible.

They passed the gamblers and turned a corner. She followed, though her heart sank seeing that they were leading her deeper into the house, away from the crowds. Dangerous, but also a good place for telling secrets. She snuck down the corridor after them. They ducked into the library, and she stood outside. Looking for an excuse if anyone saw her, she crouched on the floor where she could claim to be looking for a lost earring on the rug.

"The French are useless. Too disorganized."

"I would rather not rely on them, at any rate."

Phoebe held her breath. Could this be Deborah's uncle? The men had the accents of well-educated London gentlemen.

"What are you doing here?" someone behind her said.

She gave a start and ran her fingers through the rough wool pile of the rug. "My earring fell off. I think it rolled down here."

"And you're looking for it in the dark?" the stranger scoffed.

Phoebe raised her eyes to the man. It wasn't actually dark, but the dim oil lamps down the corridor cast long shadows. She didn't recognize him, but he was dressed in a black suit like many of the party guests, and a quizzing glass dangled from a chain on his waistcoat.

The men in the library peered out, their expressions wary. She shifted to block their view of Mushroom crouching behind her in the shadows. The dragon would only make them more suspicious.

One of the men from the library gave a familiar nod to the man in the hall. "What's all the racket out here?"

"I was just looking for a lost earring," Phoebe said.

"Sneaking off, maybe meeting up with someone?" The brute who had tripped over her leered.

She wanted to deny it, but it was better than admitting to spying. She stood and refused to speak.

"Well, if you're looking for some male companionship, we can oblige you," one of the men said.

"No," Phoebe said quickly. "I was looking for someone specific."

"You're going to hurt our feelings."

They circled around her, backing her against the wall.

"Stop it!" Phoebe stomped at one of the men's feet. He dodged and laughed.

Mushroom launched himself at the first brute's face. The man scrambled back, screaming and flailing, but the other two closed in on her. One of them pinned her arms against the wall.

"Dragon-linked are you?" he asked, leaning close to her face.

And then he gasped. His breath came out in a white fog, and his eyes went wide.

His companion backed away from him, but ice slithered and crackled along the walls. All three of the men scattered down the corridor. Mushroom trotted back to Phoebe, clutching a quizzing glass in his teeth.

Lord Westing ran up to her. He looked for a moment like he would chase the men, but then his eyes found hers.

"Did they harm you?"

She shook her head, her whole body trembling, and not from the cold. "But they would have. Thank you."

He folded her into an embrace, and though she was startled, she quickly returned it, clasping his coat with shaking hands.

"What were you thinking?" Westing quickly stepped back, his face slightly red.

Phoebe flushed, too. She could not have put herself—or Lord Westing—in a more compromising position if she tried. Her father and mother would die of humiliation. Max would be furious. Her sisters would be shunned.

She stepped back and scooped Mushroom into her arms. "I couldn't find anyone else, and I heard them talking about dragons. I think they were Luddites. I had to find out... They were trying to get help from the French, but they said they were on their own."

Westing regarded her seriously. "That was foolish but brave. It sounds like you had more luck than I did tonight in Blackerby's ridiculous quest. I hope he will be satisfied with it."

He raised a hand as though he would touch her face, but then he lowered it and offered his arm. "We need to find your brother."

"How did you find me?"

"I've been watching the gamblers. Listening. I saw you sneak off on your own and was afraid you might be up to mischief."

Phoebe wanted to be angry at his teasing, but she was only grateful that he had followed her. That did not stop the fact that everything about this situation was improper. She should not have been spying. She should not have been standing alone with Lord Westing. She should not wish that he *had* touched her face, want to feel his fingertips on her skin. Improper. Yet something in her whispered that it would feel right.

She accepted his arm, and he guided her back toward the gardens. The music had stopped, and loud voices carried on the night air. Westing's dragon hissed. Phoebe and Westing exchanged a concerned look.

Max hurried up to them. "There you are. Come quick! There's a riot!"

They followed him back to the garden. The shouting grew louder.

Captain Parry and several of the male guests and footmen were engaged in a fistfight with a group of ruffians like those who had been watching the house. Several of the attackers carried the lances of Luddites.

Eliza looked on, her hands to her mouth. Moreau had swooned, but no one paid him any mind. Lady Millicent's eyes were wide, and she clutched Lady Amelia, who for once looked ruffled. One of the Luddites took a step toward them. Lady Millicent's lip curled up in disgust. She stepped in front of Lady Amelia and shoved her folded fan into the man's face like a blade. He staggered back, holding his bleeding nose. Phoebe nodded her approval.

Both Eliza's and Lady Millicent's dragons dove at the ruffians, landing at times to dig teeth into scalps or backs. Eliza's dragon spewed steaming water into the face of one attacker, who howled in pain.

Captain Parry leveled his opponent with a swift punch. Westing and Max rushed forward, Westing's dragon leaping from his shoulder to join the chaos overhead. Farris, appearing from the direction of the stables, barreled into the ruffians, knocking several to the ground.

"You're under arrest in the name of the king!" Farris shouted, his voice carrying over the yells, thuds, and groans.

Most of the ruffians stopped fighting when faced with the enormous Bow Street Runner. Westing grabbed the arm of one man who tried to sneak away.

Phoebe hurried to Eliza's side.

"What happened?" Phoebe asked.

Eliza was trembling. Her dragon landed on her shoulder and rubbed its face against hers. She placed a hand on its back. "They broke through from the stables."

"They were shouting about magic and aristocrats," Lady Millicent added, her voice high-pitched. "One of them threw a rotten cabbage at me. It's just like France!"

Phoebe suspected it wasn't that severe yet. But her brother, Westing, and the other gentlemen limped back from their encounter with bleeding knuckles and swollen lips. Max would have a nasty bruise under one eye. The ratafia swam in Phoebe's stomach, too warm and sweet. The Luddites were on the path to the revolution they wanted.

"Westing!" Lady Millicent threw herself into the viscount's arms and then recoiled, rubbing chilled hands and regarding him with fear.

The cold rolling off him reached Phoebe. He looked at Lady Millicent with disdain and, Phoebe thought, a trace of hurt in his eyes at her reaction to his magic.

"We need to escort all of you home," he said. "It's not safe here for anyone dragon-linked."

Chapter Twenty-Two

AFTER SPENDING TOO much of the night going over the Luddite disturbance with Lord Blackerby, Westing called the next morning in Grosvenor Street. Just to check on Miss Hart. It seemed the proper thing to do.

She met him in the drawing-room. Her normally bright eyes were dull with fatigue or worry. He wished he could say they were out of danger.

"I wanted to be sure you were well," he said. Impulsively, he added, "I wonder if you might be allowed to walk out with me? Just on the street here. The fresh air will do you good. Mr... Farris, I believe it is, could accompany us."

Miss Hart looked uncertain, but she nodded her agreement. Westing escorted her out toward the square, Farris a respectful distance behind.

Carriages rumbled past while women walked little, barking dogs or laughing children along the sidewalk. Vendors sold flowers and fruit from baskets and carts, and street sweepers stood with their brooms ready to clear the dirt and horse leavings from the path of anyone willing to pay.

Many of the passersby—gentle and low—cast nervous looks at Westing and Miss Hart. Two dragon-linked people strolling along Grosvenor Street while the Luddites were at large. Miss Hart squirmed under their dark glances and tightened her grip on his arm.

"I'm so glad you were there last night," she said. "When I saw the ice crackling down the corridor, I knew I was safe."

He repressed an urge to pull her closer. How different she was from Lady Millicent, who recoiled in horror from his magic.

She flushed under his gaze and looked down. "Can you truly just… just use your attunement whenever you like?"

She made it sound like such an accomplishment, but Westing knew that came from her inexperience. He glanced around at the street vendors and paid a woman for an apple. He concentrated just enough cold to chill it then handed it to Phoebe.

"Oh, how delightful!"

She took a bite of the apple and closed her eyes in bliss. Westing, however, couldn't take his gaze from her lips, now curled into a smile, very soft looking and almost as pink as the blush on the apple.

"It must be wonderful to be able to control it," she said wistfully.

"It's essential," he said more sharply than he meant to. "For me, anyway."

He held out his hand for the apple, and she placed it gently in his palm. He concentrated again, and cold seeped through the apple, turning its juice to ice and splitting the apple open.

"You see?" he asked quietly.

She took the apple from him, her hand brushing his, and her touch sent warmth rushing up his arm despite the chill of the apple. "Yes. It could be dangerous."

He nodded and pulled his hands away. He never wanted to hurt anyone again with his touch.

"I wonder, in your case," he said carefully, not wanting to overstep but hoping to help her understand. "I wonder if your hesitation makes it more difficult for you to use your ability."

"My hesitation?"

"I don't mean to be impolite, but it seems that you are almost embarrassed to be dragon-linked."

She looked away, and he wondered if he had said too much, taken a liberty of familiarity that he had no right to.

"You're correct," she said. "You must understand, growing up away from the city, dragons are not a common sight. Maybe an older one, rumored to be sleeping under some hill, but not young ones, playing about and… and giving people powers that some still feel are unnatural."

"The Church has been very clear that dragons are part of the natural order."

"Yes, but it's one thing for someone to say it's natural and another for people to accept something that for a long time only belonged to the few, and those of a class wholly separated from themselves."

He thought that over. "Music, however, is perfectly acceptable for a young lady."

"Just so." She bit her lower lip, and once again, Westing had to use all his self-control not to stare. Or to brush his thumb over its softness. She looked to him. "You think if I was not so embarrassed by my abilities, I would be able to use them better?"

"Embarrassed. Or frightened." He glanced down, having trouble meeting her frank brown eyes. "There was a time when I could not summon cold, no matter how I tried."

"What happened? How did you learn?"

"I… I had to, if not forgive myself, at least accept that I could not undo what I had done."

"What you had done?"

He drew a deep breath, the words catching in his throat. He

never spoke of it, but maybe he could trust her gentle heart. "Joshua's hand."

"His…" her eyes widened. "Oh. Poor Joshua. I see. Cold can be dangerous." He expected her to turn away from him in disgust, kind-hearted as she was, but she just regarded him with sympathy. "I cannot believe you did it on purpose."

"Of course not! But I should have been more careful."

"You were not very old, I imagine."

"A youth. But I should have understood the… the responsibility that comes with such an ability. Joshua wanted me to make him a little bauble of ice. He trusted me, and I hurt him."

"You made a mistake. A sad one, it is certain, but Joshua has clearly forgiven you, and he still looks to you with admiration."

"I know. I could almost bear it better if he resented me, at least a little."

"I think he is setting you an excellent example. My father always said that forgiveness is a step of healing, like pulling out a splinter. And that includes forgiveness of self."

"A religious man must say such things, I suppose."

"Or a wise man," she returned.

Westing's father had certainly not been so forgiving. He already resented that his second son and not his first was dragon-linked and that his attunement was not a useful one for helping the estate like earth or water. Had he also been unwise?

Something brushed Westing's pocket. His hand shot out, and he caught the wrist of a filthy child with his pocketbook clutched in its hand.

"Nice try, scamp, but you'll have to return that."

Miss Hart's eyes widened in horror at the appearance of the child, but then her face softened, and she said, "Oh, you're not going to turn her in, are you?"

Westing glanced down at the child, and it—she?—stared defiantly back. He wanted to release her wrist, afraid his temper would overcome him and he would hurt the child with cold, but he also had a duty not to let the theft go unpunished.

"I can't turn her loose to pick another pocket."

"Oh, of course, you must not!" She crouched down to be level with the girl and smiled at her. "We must find her a... a school! Or some other positive, reforming institution. Just because we are having difficulties, it does not mean we should forget about the troubles of others."

The waif's eyes widened, and she shared a confused look with Westing, which made his mouth twitch in amusement. Dragon hopped down to pace a circle around the child, and her mouth opened in childish wonder.

"You cannot just take a girl from the streets," Westing said reluctantly. "She probably has a family."

"Oh, you sound just like Max! But a family that makes her steal and shift for herself? If they cannot afford to keep her, they might be happy to see her safely placed in a school. Do you have a family, dear?"

The girl, still looking extremely skeptical, said, "I ain't got no family, begging your pardon, miss. I only got me crew and the dimber damber what makes me 'unt dummee for 'im."

Miss Hart looked to Westing for a translation.

"Er, she does not have a proper family, I gather. Only an association of thieves that requires her to pick pockets."

Miss Hart's eyes hardened at that. "That settles it. We cannot send her back to such a life!"

"It is terrible, but I'm not certain we ought to get involved. It's not our proper place."

"Oh, nonsense. I'm not at all certain that what is proper is the same as what is right. We can find the girl... What is your name, child?"

"Molly, miss."

Miss Hart looked to Westing. "We can find Molly an apprenticeship with a kind woman somewhere out of the city, away from its wicked influences. If not, you must know what life awaits her."

She gave him a knowing and unblushing stare, which made him flush a little. He had not suspected her to be aware of such worldly matters. His father would simply have turned the girl over to the authorities. But perhaps his father had not been so wise. What was proper was not always what was right. He looked down at the girl, whose forehead was drawn in confusion, though she did not look frightened. Probably not understanding that her world was about to be turned on its head. Westing felt a moment of sympathy with her.

"I suppose we cannot allow that," he said.

Miss Hart beamed at him, and something melted inside his chest. His heart of ice or stone?

"I knew you could not be so unfeeling as some!" she said.

He felt like a cad, knowing he was probably at least as unfeeling. "Well, what do you propose to do with the child?"

"I will take her to Aunt Seraphina," she said, and Westing wished he could see the look on Lady Jasper's face when presented with her new charge. Then Miss Hart gave him an arch look. "And we will await you to find her a suitable school or apprenticeship."

"Oh," he said, seeing that he was to play a part in the farce. He glanced back at Farris, who looked like he was trying not to laugh.

"Certainly, you have all sorts of connections and people, don't you?" Miss Hart asked. "People who would be happy to please you?"

He could not deny it. "In the country, I suppose. But does the girl want to be snatched from the city?"

"Well, child?" Miss Hart asked. "Would you like to leave the city? To go live somewhere warm and have plenty of food and something good to do?"

The girl looked sullen for a moment, then she burst into tears. "Yes, mistress, please!"

Miss Hart wrapped the girl in an embrace, no doubt permanently soiling her gown, and soothed the child's dirty hair. "There, there. Everything is fine now."

And, Westing realized, for that girl, it probably was. He felt a moment's apprehension that the girl might be a Luddite spy, but the Luddites did not seem so subtle.

Miss Hart urged the girl to stop crying and follow her to her aunt's. Westing would have the enjoyment of seeing Lady Jasper's reaction after all.

Chapter Twenty-Three

As they walked, the street urchin clinging to Miss Hart's hand, Westing grew quiet, ignoring the occasional curious glance shot their way. Miss Hart seemed oblivious to them, at least.

"What are you thinking about so seriously?" she asked.

"I am glad this child will have a better situation in life, but you realize there are so very many more out there?"

She sighed. "Yes, of course, I do."

"And are you going to try to rescue all of them?"

"I would if I could!" she said fiercely. "Of course, I know I cannot. If only everyone was as good as you and willing to help —then the work would not be so heavy."

"I imagine you are right."

"Though once you've found a good place for one such child, it may open up more avenues next time."

"Next time?" Westing asked, fighting the urge to laugh. "You plan to rescue every child who tries to pick my pocket?"

"Certainly! If someone in need falls into my way, I will help them."

Now he did laugh. "Miss Hart, you will make me the target for every ambitious young 'dummee hunter' in London!"

She laughed at this, too. "Then perhaps you should find a less wearisome way to funnel them out of the city."

This sobered him again. It was outside of his sphere of duty, trying to rescue London's street children, but he did have a few ideas of where the girl might have a happier and more useful life, perhaps apprenticed to a weaver or seamstress. And with many country people moving to the city for opportunities there and finding the streets paved with misery instead of gold, could not he do something in his district to make life there more appealing, more full of opportunities, and stop the flood of people leaving? Perhaps even make a place for those needing to come back?

With those heavy thoughts in his mind, they reached Lady Jasper's residence.

Lady Jasper was not at home, so Miss Hart left Westing in the drawing-room and hurried her young charge upstairs to bathe. Lucky, Westing thought, that Lady Jasper would at least see a cleaner version of the waif.

As he sat, he noticed one of Miss Charity's books lying beside the sofa. Did Miss Hart read them? She could not have helped recognizing his caricature. But she did not believe his heart was stone. She showed no fear or distrust of him, even knowing that he had hurt Joshua. In the light of her warmth, some of the lingering memories of his father's harshness melted away.

The child that Miss Hart reintroduced to the drawing-room was still too thin and had a vulgar way of staring around that betrayed her origins, but she looked better for having been bathed and clothed with her hair groomed into a braid. At least she looked like a girl now. Like a punch to his stomach, he realized her boyish appearance had probably been a form of protection, and his throat tightened at the thought of the responsibility that came with taking that thin protection away. He wondered, as he so often did in Miss Hart's presence, what his father would think of all this. He was surprised and disconcerted to find that he didn't care.

And when Lady Jasper returned and wept over the plight of the poor waif, saying, of course, they would shelter her, Westing began to think his father had been very unwise indeed.

~

When Westing returned home, his butler said somberly, "Horace Langley awaits you in your study, my lord." His proper facade cracked for a moment, and he added, "I am sorry, my lord, but he insisted."

Westing nodded stiffly, a cold feeling creeping over him. Uncle Horace could be very insistent. And his presence in London boded ill for Joshua. Miss Hart could rescue unknown waifs from the street, but Westing could not protect his own brother. He strode into his study.

Uncle Horace sat at Westing's desk. He had placed the seal back on the left side and was shuffling through the drawers. Uncle Horace shared the Langley white-blond hair, though his face was flaccid and drained of color. Westing wasn't sure Horrible Horace could smile if he wished to. The sight of the man turned his stomach. He hoped he would age better than his uncle had.

Joshua sat very still on one of the chairs, his face cast down and Tom on his lap.

"A cat, nephew?" Horace said without preamble. "The entire town thinks you have gone mad."

Joshua clung to Tom, his eyes bright with unshed tears and righteous indignation. "He wants us to throw Tom out. And he's not even healed."

Westing took off his hat. "There you have it, uncle. We would be poor hosts to thrust out an injured guest. The cat must stay."

Horace rolled his eyes and pushed himself to his feet. "That is not the only reason I have come. I hear disturbing things about your behavior regarding… females."

"Females?" Westing wanted to laugh at the way his uncle said it, but he couldn't risk outright offending the man for Joshua's sake.

"I care little what you do if you are discreet, but these rumors about finding places for some brats of yours? It sickens me."

That surprised a laugh out of Westing, but he quickly composed himself.

His uncle glared. "And this dragon-linked upstart you have made your latest flirt is unacceptable. I thought I made that clear. She is too low to marry, but you cannot trifle with a girl whose aunt is well-connected."

"If her aunt is well-connected, I see no reason why she should not be as well."

"You cannot be serious. The gossip about her odd behavior is wild enough to tell me she is not fit to be the next Viscountess Westing."

"Gossip!" Westing sneered.

"Yes, gossip, nephew. We have a duty to maintain our respectability, and you especially as the head of the family, however little you may be fit for it. The name of Langley cannot be dragged through the gutter by lesser persons."

Westing thought of the Stone Knight. "No. We ought to do that ourselves, eh, uncle? We are so disgustingly proud, we raise ourselves up to be mocked. It would do us some good to be humbled."

"Is your position a joke to you? You *are* an unfit guardian, as your father knew. I will take this boy in hand and raise him to be a proper Langley, no matter what his mother is."

Westing pulled off his gloves. His skin was as cold as the

frost on a January lake. "Do so, and nothing will stop me from trying to persuade Miss Hart to marry me."

"Then you will never see your brother again."

"West?" Joshua whimpered, his voice unsteady. "I'll let Tom go."

Westing tossed the gloves aside. His fingers ached with the cold running deep into his bones. Ice was pain. Destruction. If he lashed out against his uncle with his magic, though, he risked being branded a traitor by his peers, and then the remainder of his family would lose everything. The chill felt like it would splinter his bones. Ice did that. It found little cracks and broke them open, severing stones, battering ruins, crumbling mountains.

And Horace Langley had one very obvious fault line.

"Very well, uncle. If I am not responsible for Joshua, there is nothing to stop me from following my fancies. You know, I avoided most of the pranks the other boys played at Eton. Didn't want to disappoint Father. But I stored up some excellent ideas."

Joshua stared at him, wide-eyed, and Horace's smirk faded.

"I will begin," Westing said, "by freeing the ostriches at the Tower menagerie and driving them about town like carriage horses. Then I will put them in wigs and set them loose in Parliament."

Horace's eyes bugged.

"And that reminds me," Westing went on. "I once saw the other boys dress up a monkey in robes and release it in the master's office. Wouldn't it be splendid to array a whole troop of monkeys in court dress and introduce them to Buckingham Palace?"

Horace's face had gone bright red. "Don't talk nonsense!"

"I'm not finished. Let me tell you my long-term plans. Miss Hart has a very generous nature, you see, and it has inspired me. I shall turn this home into an asylum for the dirtiest street urchins you can dream of. They'll be a bit hard on the furniture, but what's that compared to knowing that the Langley family is good enough to bring the poor of London right into Berkeley Square?"

"This house—"

"Is mine, and I will do with it as I please. I am the head of the Langley family, after all. I will give each child a choice of pets, too: cats, dogs, birds. The smell will be a bit much, but the neighbors will adapt."

"You want to make a mockery of your family legacy?"

"I will make what I wish of my family legacy, and there are certain portions of it that need improving." He picked up the family seal, twirled it around his fingers, and slammed it back on the desk exactly where he wanted it. "I don't care what anyone else thinks. But I do care about Joshua, and I will not let you use him as a weapon against me. As long as he is in my care, I will avoid situations that might land me in gaol or render the house unsuitable for his upbringing. Remove him, and I don't care if the name of Langley becomes a byword in all of England. Let us say Joshua is a civilizing influence on me and leave him where he is."

Horace looked like he was going to scoff at this, but then he regarded the ragged cat snuggled in Joshua's arms, and his resolve faltered. "Your father would—"

"No doubt whatever you wish to say is true, but you may keep it to yourself. Now, shall I have a servant air out a room for you, or will you be leaving immediately?"

"I would not sleep one night under this roof if it were the last one in London."

Westing bowed stiffly. "I take it, then, that I need not invite you to the wedding?"

Horace's eyes narrowed. "You're going to marry that common, upstart nobody?"

Dragon hissed and stalked toward Uncle Horace, who pulled back in alarm.

"I am going to marry Miss Phoebe Hart, if she'll have me," Westing said. "And if you ever again say a word against her—whether she marries me or not—you'll find yourself in an ice block bobbing in the Thames."

Uncle Horace gave an inarticulate cry of rage and stormed out of the room. Dragon hopped after him, spitting ice in his wake.

Westing looked to Joshua and wondered how much of a poor example he had just set.

"I'm glad you're going to marry Miss Hart," Joshua said, his eyes bright with admiration. "Can we really have an ostrich?"

Chapter Twenty-Four

PHOEBE SAT READING Miss Charity's novel in the library, but without as much humor as usual. Her character seemed a little silly, she thought, as the girl wandered about with her glowing orb. Sometimes she lit the way for the knights, but other times she wandered blindly into trouble. It irked Phoebe that some unknown person watched what she did and mocked it. She was doing the best she could, but how could she tell that to the anonymous author? Everyone must think her a fool.

And if Miss Charity was watching everyone in secret, who else might be? Jamie still reported no sign of the spying man, and Phoebe found his absence almost as disturbing as his presence had been. Lord Blackerby told her they should keep about their normal activities in the face of the Luddite troubles, so her aunt was planning an outing to Vauxhall Gardens. Phoebe had once been excited to see the garden's walkways and fireworks, but now the idea left a heavy feeling in her stomach.

The butler came to find her. "Are you at home, Miss Hart?"

He held out the tray. Phoebe was afraid it might be Mr.

Moreau, whom she did not trust after the incident at his house party. But it was Lord Westing.

She took the card, hoping the butler could not see how she treasured it. "Yes. I'll be down presently."

The butler bowed and withdrew, and Phoebe quickly resorted to the mirror to be sure her hair was in order. Her cheeks were flushed, but she hoped it made her look pretty and not like a silly schoolgirl. Having done her best at the mirror, she walked as calmly as she could to the drawing-room.

Lord Westing sat studying his quizzing glass idly, the drawing-room doors wide open for propriety. Phoebe's aunt wasn't home, and Deborah couldn't serve as a duenna.

"Ask my brother to join us, please," she whispered to the butler as she walked past him. Max would have to serve as chaperone.

"Lord Westing, how good of you to call," she said, extending a hand, which he took and held for a moment before bowing over it and kissing her fingertips. Her breath caught at the gentle touch of his lips. His eyes met hers, and she couldn't look away from their pale blue.

Dragon glided off his shoulder and landed in front of Mushroom. The two dragons circled each other then butted heads.

"How is the beneficiary of your charity?" Westing finally said.

"Molly is a bit untame," Phoebe answered with a nervous titter. "Uncle pays little heed, but I think my poor aunt is overwhelmed. She didn't have children, you see, so she doesn't know that they can all be wild at times. I'm sure Joshua was."

"Always in trouble," Westing agreed. "Though never anything serious, as long as cats aren't involved."

Phoebe laughed. "But he seems to adore them."

"Yes, Joshua has been too kind to Tom. He's becoming fat

and lazy. I suppose he'll be returning with us after the Season to Westing Hall. It's in Dorset, you know. Near the coast."

"It sounds lovely. Do you think you'll find a place there for Molly? How healthy it will be for her to be out of the city."

Westing was silent for a long moment, and Phoebe struggled to guess what he might be thinking. Did he regret offering to help her?

Finally, he said, "Would you like to be out of the city?"

"I've enjoyed some of its amusements, but I miss the quiet of the country."

"I have trouble imagining you being quiet."

She smiled. "Perhaps quiet is not the right word. More, able to go on in my own way."

"You chafe at London's rules?"

"Its unfamiliarity, I think. I will always feel out of place in a city."

"Do you suppose you would enjoy Dorset?"

Phoebe glanced at him uncertainly. "It sounds lovely. I would like to visit the sea."

"Then perhaps you shall. Sometime soon."

Phoebe's tongue felt all tied in knots. Was Westing truly hinting what she thought he was? Did she want him to? Yes, oh, yes. She would feel safe and cherished in his arms. But would people look down on him for making such an ineligible match? Would she always be out of place by his side?

"I do have good news for Molly," he went on.

He motioned to the sofa, and they sat next to each other. Phoebe was very aware of the warmth of his presence and the masculine scent of his coat. His dragon hopped up to nudge her hand with its head, and it allowed her to scratch behind its wings.

"In fact," Westing said, a glimmer in his eyes, "I have found a girls' school that could take several new pupils. In case any more pickpockets come my way."

Phoebe laughed. "You are too good!"

"I've been thinking that something ought to be done for Jamie as well. I know he is of service to you here, but he is a bright lad, and if he could settle down to schooling, he might excel."

"Yes, I imagine he would. I wonder if he would like it."

"If not, I would sponsor him in an apprenticeship of some kind. Brainy Jamie ought not to be wasted on the streets."

"No indeed. It is so kind of you to take the trouble."

"You have reminded me where my duty lies—not just on the grounds of my estate." His lips twitched in a smile. "Besides, you make it easy with your unique way of bringing charity cases to my attention. How much longer do you suppose you will need the lad's services?"

"Well, as long as I'm in London, and I suppose I'm here—" she stopped herself. She could not say *until I find a husband.* "Well, until my aunt grows tired of me."

"I cannot imagine that happening quickly."

Phoebe smiled and shook her head, freeing an errant curl to tumble to her forehead.

Westing reached up and brushed it back for her. His touch sent a pleasant shiver over her skin. Their eyes met, and they stared for several heartbeats without saying anything. Phoebe's gaze drifted to his lips, and she leaned closer.

"Phoebe!" Max's voice came from down the corridor as a warning.

Phoebe gave a guilty start, and Westing quickly looked away. Max's presence was perhaps needed, but why did he sound so urgent? He couldn't have seen the moment that passed between Westing and her from the corridor.

"Er, Phoebs, watch out—" Max's voice was closer now, but a rush of wings preceded him.

Rahab glided into the drawing-room, coming to rest on the

mantle of the fireplace. Phoebe gritted her teeth and glanced at Westing, whose forehead wrinkled in confusion.

"Is that the rogue dragon?" he asked. "You have tamed it?"

"No. Well, it might have been lost for a short time, but it's not rogue. It's linked to... someone I know."

"Does Lord Blackerby know? He had many questions about the creature."

"She desires privacy."

"The dragon-linked lose a certain degree of privacy. What is behind this secrecy?"

He watched her, his face unreadable again, though there was a trace of something—Anger? Hurt?—in his eyes. She felt her color rising and looked away.

"Miss Hart, I would hope... I would hope you would feel free to tell me anything. Perhaps if you needed help or advice?"

She longed to confide everything in him—to ask if she was doing right—but it was not her secret to tell. "Do not ask me to say more."

His expression stiffened, and his eyes became more guarded. Phoebe's heart ached, but she could not break her promise to Deborah.

"I wish you would trust me," he whispered.

"I wish *you* would trust that I know the right thing to do."

"But do you?" His voice came out rough. "You act with your heart instead of your head. It's fine when you're offering charity to street urchins, but not with matters that may affect the safety of the nation."

Phoebe paled. Did she have a higher duty? Maybe it was right thing to tell Westing everything. She wanted to. She did not want to see the anger in his eyes when just a few moments before there had been something much more tender there. But Deborah had put her safety in Phoebe's hands, and they did not know where spies might be lurking. "I will not be a betrayer. Don't... I beg you, don't say anything to anyone."

He hesitated, his expression pained. "You have a duty. We all do. Do you not realize what danger you may have put yourself in?"

Phoebe's eyes welled with tears. "Please, say no more."

Westing's face hardened. "You leave me with little choice."

With that, he turned and stormed out past Max, who had watched the whole thing from the doorway.

"I tried to stop the dragon, Phoebs," Max said when Westing was gone. "Molly let her out."

Phoebe shut her eyes against the stinging burn of her tears. "I do not blame you. Or Molly. Secrets will not keep forever. Especially not in London, it seems."

Deborah arrived in the doorway, pale and out of breath. When she saw the scene, she burst into tears. Phoebe was annoyed at her for a moment, but the girl gasped out, "I'm sorry for causing trouble, and after you've been so good to me."

Phoebe's heart softened. "You did not ask for this. I only hope you're not in more danger now."

"Will that man turn me in? Will the Luddites find me?"

Phoebe sighed and sank against the sofa, her chest burning with repressed sobs. "I don't know."

Chapter Twenty-Five

WESTING STORMED THROUGH THE STREETS, hardly looking where he was going. People sensed the wisdom of clearing out of his way. He was certain he would accidentally freeze someone if they touched him, but all he could do was keep moving. The tears in Miss Hart's eyes clawed his heart to shreds, but how could she ask him not to tell Blackerby that the dragon they had been looking for—maybe some of the answers they had been looking for—were right under their noses?

Had Miss Hart been taken in by some conspirator? A female, he gathered, but women could be dangerous, too. He alternately wanted to shake Miss Hart for being so foolish and hold her to protect her from whatever the consequences might be.

But she would not let him protect her. He had imagined she trusted him. He had hoped her kind heart might be one that could love him. Stupid notion. Outside of Joshua's boyish devotion, no one had ever loved Westing. Ice and cold were not elements meant for love. But they were ideally suited for duty.

Miss Hart had pushed him away and into an impossible position. He was honor-bound to tell Blackerby where the rogue dragon was, even if it made Miss Hart his enemy. And if she would not talk to him—even as a friend—he could not help her.

He resisted the urge to slam his fist into something and stopped. He stood alone, even in bustling London.

Blackerby would likely be at Whitehall or Bow Street. That meant that if Westing left his card in Grosvenor Square, he could buy himself a little time to decide what to say to Blackerby. Because even if Miss Hart wanted nothing from Westing, he still had to find a way to protect her.

His course decided, he turned for Grosvenor Square, filled with relief when the butler announced that the earl was not at home. Westing left his card and walked back to Berkeley Square.

Joshua bounded up to meet him, though his smile faded when he saw Westing's expression. "West? Has something happened? Did you see Miss Hart? Is she unwell?"

Westing's first instinct was to shoo Joshua away. Hide his pain. It was what his father would have done. Put up a cold facade. But his father had not been wise.

West sat heavily at the desk and rolled his family seal on the worn wood. Dragon rubbed his head under Westing's chin then curled up in his lap with a discontented groan.

"I am worried about our friend," Westing told his brother. "London is dangerous right now for those who are dragon-linked, and her kindness may have led her to help someone she shouldn't trust."

Joshua looked confused. "Someone might hurt her because she's kind? That's terrible! You should plant him a facer."

"Not if 'he' is a 'she.'" Westing chuckled despite his pain. "Where have you learned boxer's slang?"

"One of the grooms. But you are going to defend her, aren't you? Even against a mean lady?" He wrinkled his nose. "Is it Lady Millicent?"

"No, it is not. I'll help Miss Hart if I can." He realized this was one of the lessons his brother needed to learn that would not come from a book. "We cannot control what other people do, though, and we cannot take away the consequences of their choices. We cannot force them to trust us."

"I'll tell her she should trust you. I can't think why she wouldn't."

Westing forced a smile at his brother. "Thank you, Josh."

"Mr. Langley!" came Sudbury's voice from the corridor. Close enough to have overheard everything. "We are not done with geometry."

"Back to your studies," Westing said.

"Very well. But we are going to see the fireworks tonight, aren't we? You promised."

Westing's heart was far from fireworks—he had offered to take Joshua because Miss Hart was going to be there—but he nodded. "If you behave."

Sudbury peeked into the study to find his charge. As he led the boy away, he gave Westing an odd, triumphant look that left Westing with a deep sense of unease.

Chapter Twenty-Six

LONDON'S LUSTER HAD TARNISHED, and it now felt like a prison where Phoebe was trapped with Lord Westing's anger and disappointment and the problem of Deborah's safety.

She kept the first to herself, but she worried over the second with her aunt, brother, and Deborah.

"We have to move Miss Sloan," Max said. "For her safety and the household's."

"Hide her from Lord Westing, you mean?" Phoebe imagined his cold fury when he realized the trick they'd played. He would see it as an unforgivable breach of her responsibilities. He might be right.

"From the Luddites," Max said. "Lord Westing seems decent, but do we know that Lord Blackerby's offices are free of spies? Even he doesn't think so."

Phoebe rubbed her forehead. "Good heavens. What have we gotten ourselves into?"

Deborah looked horrified. "I'll turn myself in to this Lord Blackerby. I never meant to put everyone in danger."

"I know you didn't mean it, dear," Phoebe said gently,

relieved that Deborah was willing to trust someone. She had to be certain that trust didn't misfire. "Perhaps the wisest thing would be to move you somewhere safe and then tell Blackerby the whole of it, keeping your location hidden. Then we could root out the Luddites without putting you in their way."

Deborah placed a hand on Rahab's back. Then she straightened, her face set in resolution. "Very well."

Max nodded his approval. "But where?"

They looked to Aunt Seraphina, who had been very thoughtful through all this. Her face brightened. "Lord Jasper has a hunting box not far from London in Hertfordshire. The staff are loyal, and his huntsman is ferocious—no one would get past him or his dogs."

"We should take her quickly," Phoebe said.

"I'll drive her," Max offered. "I'll take her in a gig or curricle so no one else knows, and since it's open, there's as little impropriety as possible. I'll simply drop her off and turn around."

Deborah smiled her thanks.

"I should go, too," Phoebe said.

"We may need you to answer questions for Lord Blackerby," Aunt Seraphina said. She added quietly, "And for Lord Jasper, too."

Phoebe swallowed and nodded. "I see. Yes. Can you bear to hide there a few days alone, Deborah? I'll join you as soon as we've dealt with their lordships."

She wasn't sure which way Deborah would go on this, but the girl held up her head and nodded. "I shall be brave."

"Good girl," Aunt Seraphina said. "Phoebe, you and I must still go to Vauxhall Gardens tonight."

"Must we?"

"I have told everyone we would be there. If we are being watched, we don't want anyone to know anything is amiss."

Phoebe shrugged her consent. They disguised Deborah in

her black veil, and after being sure no one was watching closely, Max drove her off.

As Aunt Seraphina prepared for their evening excursion, Phoebe motioned Farris aside.

"I have something important to tell Lord Blackerby. Something about the rogue dragon and the Luddites. Can you arrange for him to meet me as soon as possible—here or at Vauxhall Gardens?"

He hesitated. "My job is to protect you, miss."

"This information is dangerous. The sooner we tell him, the sooner everyone might be safe."

Farris looked pained, but he nodded his agreement. "I'll find Blackerby. You stay with your aunt."

"Of course."

Phoebe and Aunt Seraphina took a boat across the Thames to enter Vauxhall Gardens by the water gates. Phoebe did her best not to gape at the enormous rotunda, the fountain with its carved dragons spouting water, and the many groves and walks. The scent of cooking meat and dough filled the air, and the air danced with the strains from the orchestra. Mushroom hopped around and sniffed the air in excitement. Little swirls of light sprung up around Phoebe as she strolled with her aunt to the supper box they had engaged, but she didn't mind; the lights seemed to fit the mood of the place.

From their supper box, they could watch the crowds passing by. Phoebe scanned the arc of boxes and spotted Westing with his little brother. Phoebe's heart leapt, but Westing did not look her way. No, he would not.

Phoebe pretended not to notice him as she and Aunt Seraphina ate their supper, but her eyes kept drifting to him. The odd thing was, it seemed other people were watching, too. Staring at him, whispering, snickering. Phoebe could see nothing to laugh at in his dignified bearing.

"It's sad, isn't it?" Lady Millicent's voice purred next to her.

"What?" Phoebe gave a start and turned to face the smirking lady who stood just outside her box, leaning in as if exchanging friendly secrets with her.

Lady Millicent flicked her fan open and closed. "He's become a laughing stock. He was perfectly respectable before you got your grubby hands on him."

"I'm sorry," Phoebe said with forced brightness. "But I don't believe you and I have ever been properly introduced."

Millicent pinched her lips together and turned away with a huff. But Phoebe was uneasy. She had to know if she had truly harmed Lord Westing.

"Aunt Seraphina, shall we stroll the Grand Walk?"

"Certainly, my dear."

Aunt Seraphina joined her, and they walked among the fashionable set, her aunt stopping to exchange pleasantries with her acquaintances. Phoebe drifted nearer to a gaggle of gossips who were staring at Lord Westing.

"I can imagine it of some men, but him?" one woman said. "I didn't think he would lower himself so."

"It is too bad, but you know what men are. One look at a pretty face, and they forget what they owe to themselves and their families."

"His father will rise from his grave."

"And think of that younger brother of his, being raised in such debasing circumstances."

Phoebe hurried away, clinging to her aunt's side. She had known all along that Westing was above her. She had never meant to hurt him or anyone else, but she had done badly after all. She should never have come to London. Tears stung her eyes at the thought, but she followed Aunt Seraphina without looking up.

As Phoebe stumbled along, hardly watching where she was going, Mushroom suddenly became agitated, hopping and flapping his wings. Phoebe looked up, wondering if Lord

Blackerby had arrived. But it was Mr. Sudbury, Joshua's tutor, his clothes rumpled and his hair out of sorts. His face appeared red and swollen behind his spectacles.

"Miss Hart," he gasped. "I'm so glad I found you."

"What is it?" Phoebe asked, glancing at her aunt.

"It's young Joshua. He's gone missing. We're searching for him."

Phoebe's chest tightened, and she looked around at the many walkways shadowed by tall hedges. "Aunt! We must help find him."

Her aunt's eyes widened. "Yes, of course, we must. Where do we begin?"

"He went this way." Sudbury motioned them into one of the narrow, shrub-lined paths. Mushroom jumped from Phoebe's shoulder and glided ahead.

Phoebe and Aunt Seraphina followed, calling Joshua's name. Phoebe quickly became disoriented in the maze of dark turns. She lost sight of Sudbury and her aunt, but she heard a raspy croak from Mushroom ahead.

"Joshua?" Phoebe called.

"Only I, Miss Hart," Sudbury said.

Mushroom sat on his arm like an ungainly falcon.

"You have a way with dragons," Phoebe said, pausing to catch her breath.

He smiled. "In my studies, I have found the things that allure them." He slid a finger down Mushroom's spine and lifted his wing to examine it. "I don't know as much as I would like, but I am learning."

Phoebe felt uneasy at the greedy look in his eyes. A foggy feeling rested over her mind like she was too tired to think anymore. "It's a shame you don't have a dragon, then."

"Perhaps. I very nearly did, but it did not work out as planned."

Phoebe shook her head, and it felt like she was underwater. "You can't simply acquire a dragon. Everyone knows that."

"I think what everyone knows is a very small tome indeed. I likely know more about dragons than you or other people who take them for granted."

"You want to marry someone with a dragon?" She stumbled over the words, her lips numb, swollen.

"Perhaps, if I can bend her to my will. Ultimately, though, it is dragons I will bend. If not, they will have to be eliminated. Magic is simply too dangerous to be left in the hands of a few spoiled aristocrats."

Phoebe stared at him. "But, you like dragons."

He smiled, and his teeth seemed very sharp and yellow. "No, they fascinate me, as the pox might fascinate a physician. And I have learned how to turn your so-called advantage in our favor. You are linked to your dragon, you see, and what affects them also affects you."

"You can't kill dragons," Phoebe slurred.

"Not thus far. We have tried, believe me, and I have not given up hope." He chuckled, a terrible sound that echoed around her. "But we have learned that a sick dragon means a sick person."

Phoebe glanced at Mushroom, who now slumped like a limp fur shawl. "What?"

"He is poisoned. And so, my dear, are you."

She stumbled, and he caught her, guiding her she knew not where. The darkness of the hedge maze and walks folded around her, trying to drag her into sleep. She thought for a moment she saw Lord Westing's white-blond hair, and she tried to call out. But then, the nightmare turned inky, and he turned his back on her, and she was alone.

Chapter Twenty-Seven

WESTING'S mind was playing tricks on him. He thought for a moment he saw Miss Hart with Mr. Sudbury in one of the shadowy walks of Vauxhall gardens. He had to banish the lady from his thoughts.

That was hard to do when her aunt came rushing up to his box. "Oh, you've found your brother. But now I don't know where Phoebe is."

"Found my brother?" Westing glanced at Joshua, who looked equally perplexed.

"Yes. His tutor said he had wandered off. We went searching for him, and now I've lost everyone."

"Joshua was never missing." Westing stood, his legs unsteady as though he stood on a boat in a storm. "Sudbury has lured her away."

"Why would he do that?" Aunt Seraphina said. "She's no heiress."

"I'm afraid it's a deeper game than that. What happened to Blackerby's man? The redheaded giant, Farris?"

"Phoebe sent him to find Lord Blackerby. She had, uh,

something urgent to talk to him about."

Westing clenched his jaw. She had decided to trust Blackerby and not him? Well, the important thing now was to make her safe. "We'll need Blackerby. Lady Jasper, can you take charge of my brother?"

"You are going to rescue Miss Hart!" Joshua said.

"Yes, I am."

"Thank you, Lord Westing!" Lady Jasper said, putting a protective arm around Joshua.

Westing strode off for the land entrance to Vauxhall Gardens. He would need a horse. He would also need to know which direction they went.

A deeper trail of shadows caught Westing's attention. Blackerby. Thank heavens! He hurried over to see the man striding down the lane, Farris at his side.

"Blackerby!" Westing called.

"Westing," Blackerby drawled. "To what do I owe this unexpected pleasure?"

"Miss Hart."

"She seems to be in the thick of things this evening," Blackerby said.

"She's missing. She was last seen in the company of Mr. Sudbury, my brother's tutor."

Farris went pale.

Blackerby's forehead creased. "How odd. Did he have some unnatural interest in Miss Hart?"

"In dragons. He occasionally said things that made me suspect he had Luddite sympathies. I should have sent him away immediately."

"No time for regrets now," Blackerby said. "Whatever Sudbury is planning, we must act swiftly. Stand back."

Westing looked at Farris, who scrambled out of the way. Westing took a cue from the Runner and stepped back.

Blackerby closed his eyes. His dragon hopped in excited

circles. The shadows hovering around him stirred to life as if blown by an invisible wind. They revolved into a dark cyclone then shot off in different directions.

Westing stood very still, not sure what to expect. Blackerby did not move, and his dragon settled on its haunches. Farris shifted but stayed where he was. In a few minutes, the shadows whirred back to dance around Blackerby. They swirled for a few moments then settled again at his feet.

Blackerby opened his eyes. "They are heading east."

Westing stared at him. "You can watch people with your shadows?"

"It's not that sophisticated. I can track darkness, and I can also sense where the darkness cannot go."

"I don't... What does that have to do with Miss Hart?"

"Darkness is an emptiness, Westing. And light... light is a presence. It pours into the darkness. Obliterates it. To the east, I sense a trail of light. I do not know exactly where Miss Hart is, but I know which way she went." Blackerby's serious expression brightened. "Find horses, lads, and any Runners who are near. We're on the hunt."

Chapter Twenty-Eight

PHOEBE WOKE to a gentle rocking motion. She sat up with a start, sure that she was on a boat to France. Sharp pain shot through her temples and black spots flashed over her vision.

She squeezed her eyes shut and blinked. It wasn't a boat but a fine carriage with cushioned seats and heavy curtains over the windows.

Sudbury sat across from her, a glass of wine in his hand as if they were in a parlor instead of hurtling across some darkened road. He smiled faintly at her, his eyes mocking. Mushroom sprawled on the floor, his eyes glassy. Still poisoned.

"Welcome back to the world, Miss Hart."

"Where are you taking me?" Phoebe said, her voice scratchy.

"Somewhere safe."

Phoebe glimpsed darkness through a crack in the curtains. "Are we… are we going to Gretna Green?"

He laughed a dry, gritty sound like a snake rustling through dry grass. "You flatter yourself, Miss Hart. I am not interested in marrying you."

As bad as that would have been, he probably had something

worse in mind. Her hands felt clammy in her lap. She peeked out the curtain at the dark landscape illuminated in flashes by the lanterns hung on the carriage. If she threw herself out of the door, would it kill her? Maim her? If she were injured, she couldn't run.

Sudbury noticed her studying the carriage door and laughed. "Oh, don't be so dramatic. I'm not going to touch you. You'll be safe enough with me. You're just a small thread in the tapestry—and not a very bright one."

She turned to glare at him in the faint lantern light. The swollen red areas on his face had resolved into the first bloom of fresh bruises. Had he fought someone? He must have won because he was there. "Did you hurt Joshua?"

"I have no reason to. Eventually, he will fall with the rest of his family. For now, he was useful in giving me access to spy on your ilk. And his little infatuation with you let me get enough information to confirm that you were hiding my niece in Grosvenor Street."

Phoebe clenched her teeth. Then, she laughed in surprise when she understood his bruises. "The first footman is a boxing enthusiast. And Deborah's not even at the house. You've been stalking it for nothing."

He held up her mother's opal bracelet. "Not for nothing, though it was clever of you to get that street brat to lie to me."

She sat back, her head throbbing. "Why opals?"

He pulled something out of his waistcoat pocket. An opal button, though its surface had lost all luster, like a dead eye. Mushroom lifted his head at the sight of the jewel, but he flopped down again.

"I'm always looking for a more potent poison," Sudbury said. "Opal has its own magic, and when its owner dies, that magic goes out. The opal of a dead man—dead dragon-linked—may nullify dragon magic, too. I plan to experiment."

He was going to kill her. Phoebe lunged for the carriage

door. Sudbury grabbed her and slammed her back against the seat. He slapped her, though his expression was calculating, not angry. Mushroom hissed and tried to rise.

"Consider your situation, foolish girl. You can be alive or dead for my experiments, but before I allow you to die, you will reunite me with my niece."

"I won't tell you where she is."

"Perhaps not, but if you are stubborn, I will print details of how I torture you in the personal ads until she surrenders to me. Or that brother of yours turns her in. And if you think you can escape, remember that you have nowhere to run. You are ruined now."

"But I haven't done anything wrong!"

"Do you think that matters? You were last seen slipping into the darkness with a man at Vauxhall Gardens. If you show up a day or two later—in the same dress, for that matter!—society will turn its back on you as if you never existed. Your family will hide you away somewhere and never speak your name so your taint doesn't spread to the rest of them. The shame will still be there, of course, because there will be rumors. The best thing you can do for them is to disappear entirely. And there, I will help you."

Phoebe's chin quivered as the full impact of her disgrace hit her. Ruined. No matter what she did.

She had ruined everything.

She swallowed hard, determined not to cry. Or to throw up. Her stomach bubbled with the heat of shame. She pressed against the seat, wishing she *could* vanish. That everyone would forget her phenomenal failure.

Max wouldn't desert her, though.

No matter what Sudbury said or did, her brother would believe her. Stand by her. Even if she wasn't innocent.

The rest of her family, too. She did not want to bring disgrace to her sisters, but her parents would never toss her aside. They knew what was right, even if no one else did. She might not marry—the thought made her throat feel hot and thick—but she would not let Sudbury win because of what other people might think or say about her. She had to escape.

She turned her face to the curtained window, trying to make out some feature of the dark landscape. To determine where they were and what direction they were heading. Someone would try to find her. Max. Aunt Seraphina. But they would not know where to search.

She leaned her head against the side of the carriage. There was a rhythm to its movement. A back-and-forth rocking, just a little off from perfect, almost like a waltz. One-two-three, one-two-three. If only Mushroom were well, she might be able to make a light.

But what had Sudbury said at Burlington House about attunement? Mushroom had given her magic, but the element was in the person. The light was in her.

She focused on the beat of the carriage, sank into it. Let it fill her. She didn't try to direct the light, just called it to her. The glow came, not in little sparkles, but as a bright orb filling the carriage and overflowing from it. A beacon for anyone searching for her.

"What are you doing?" Mr. Sudbury smacked Phoebe across the face again, sending her head rocking to the side.

It broke her concentration, and the light dissipated like white smoke. She blinked, and her pulse throbbed in her vision. Her heartbeat. She squeezed her eyes shut. It thrummed through the ache on her face. In her head. Down her arms. A constant rhythm. She pictured light pulsing with each beat. Building. Overflowing.

A blinding flash visible through her eyelids.

Mr. Sudbury screamed. Phoebe opened her eyes. Her captor swiped at his face.

She gasped, and her breath came out in a white puff. Her

skin was chilled, her fingers numb with cold. Ice crackled across the carriage windows.

"What is happening?" Sudbury yelled, rubbing frantically at his eyes.

The horses neighed in terror, and the carriage jolted then skidded as though running on something slick.

"Slow down, you fool!" Mr. Sudbury called to the driver, but there was no response.

The carriage swung sideways, looped in a wild circle, and tilted. Phoebe jumped forward after Mushroom, who scrambled drunkenly to get to his feet. The carriage slammed onto its side, throwing everything into confusion.

Tentacles of darkness curled around the upset carriage.

Mr. Sudbury swore and kicked. Wood splintered. Phoebe found Mushroom in the darkness and confusion and wrapped him in her arms, grateful to feel his steady breathing. She pressed against the tilted floor of the carriage to stay away from Sudbury.

"Miss Hart!" Westing's voice came from outside.

Her heart soared. "I'm here!"

Someone tore away the broken door and a strong hand reached in to guide her from the wreckage. She found her feet, blinked at the faint light of a fallen carriage lantern, and then Westing's arms were around her.

"Are you unharmed?" His voice was gruff against her ear.

She wanted desperately to relax into the safety of his arms, but if she had been an embarrassment to his station before, she was certainly one now.

"Where is Sudbury?" Blackerby called.

Phoebe reluctantly stepped away from Westing, still cradling Mushroom, and hummed a shaky tune, producing a weak orb of light overhead. It was enough to brighten the black night.

The men spread out, searching the road and beating the

hedgerows to turn up any sign of the man. They returned, shaking their heads.

The driver had escaped the crash with only a broken arm, but he protested loudly that he knew nothing about the man who had hired him.

Sudbury had vanished.

Phoebe stopped her song, and the light blinked out, leaving them only with the dim glow of the one unbroken carriage lantern.

"Can't you track his dark emotions?" Westing asked Blackerby.

Phoebe looked to Blackerby in surprise, but the earl shook his head.

"I cannot." Blackerby sounded vexed and a little worried. "He doesn't have any."

"What do you mean?" Westing asked. "Fear? Anger?"

"Nothing. Either this man does not feel, or he is not greatly upset about the events of tonight."

Westing swore under his breath. "At least we have Miss Hart safe." He turned and took her free hand. "When I realized you were gone, I wanted to flog myself for hiring Sudbury. Putting you and Joshua both in danger."

"You could not have known," Phoebe said. She needed to pull her hand away. She had to let Westing go.

"I should have trusted you, though. I should have stayed close to you."

He drew her in, but she resisted.

"Miss Hart?" he asked.

"Don't you understand?" She lowered her voice, aware of the Runners lingering nearby. "Mr. Sudbury has ruined me."

The shock and outrage on Westing's face shook Phoebe, and she had to look away before his surprise turned to disappointment. To disgust. It would be bad enough from the rest of the *ton*. From Westing, it would break her.

But he gently squeezed her hand. "I'm sorry he hurt you." His fingers were icy, but she didn't want to let go. "I'm so sorry I couldn't protect you." He stepped in front of her and knelt. "At the very least, let me offer you the protection of my name."

Tears burned her eyes. "No, my lord—"

"I will be whatever you want from me. Husband, if you'll have me. Or guardian. Friend." His voice hardened. "And I will find that monster and freeze the flesh off his bones strip by strip."

Phoebe gasped and clutched his hand harder to cut him off. "Oh, no! You don't have to… my lord, he didn't… injury me. But my reputation is beyond repair. You are… are dear to me. I could not bear to sully yours."

Westing's eyes glittered. "*My* reputation! My dear, lovely girl, do you realize that half of Town has heard of the monstrous feline roaming my house and thinks I've gone mad? And every member of the *ton* who's awake has noticed the brats I've been finding homes for and thinks I am the most prolific and unashamed rake. Not that either of us should care what they think, but I assure you, they would only wonder how you could stoop to accept me."

Phoebe choked on a half-laugh, half-sob. "Then I *have* ruined you."

"My heart, you have saved me, if only you will say you love me, too, so I can get off the ground and kiss you." He grinned. "You've ruined my reputation; it's the only honorable thing to do."

All of Phoebe's objections rose to her throat, but the only word that came to her lips was, "Yes."

Westing stood and scooped her into his arms, making her drop Mushroom. Her heart fluttered so wildly, she found it hard to breathe, so she closed her eyes and melted into the feeling of safety, like Westing could shield her from every doubt and worry and fear. And then his lips found hers, warm and a little rough as he kissed her again and again. She dissolved into it, dizzy and flying free.

"What was Sudbury after?" Blackerby's voice came as if from somewhere far off.

Westing paused kissing her long enough to say, "Be quiet and go away."

"It's not your honeymoon yet, lovestruck fools." Blackerby whacked Westing with his cane. "Snap out of it. What the devil was Sudbury's plan? What did he say to you, Miss Hart?"

She blinked, trying to bring her mind back to earth. She was not singing, but a bright orb floated overhead. She retrieved Mushroom, who was looking more alert now. "Sudbury wanted Deborah Sloan."

"Ah," Blackerby said. His dark eyebrows drew together. "Who on earth is that?"

"I believe she is his niece. She escaped from him because he wanted to use her magic against the other dragon-linked. The rogue dragon is hers. I didn't know it when I found her, but I promised to keep her hidden. Safe." She glanced at Westing. "I could not break my word, but I did convince her to seek Lord Blackerby's help."

Westing slowly broke into a grin. "So, she was another of your waifs?"

Phoebe smiled, too, but then grew serious again and explained Sudbury's plans.

Blackerby swore long and eloquently when she told them about the Queen's Drawing-room, and his face turned grim at the news that Sudbury could poison dragons.

Phoebe looked down at Mushroom, who blinked at her, his eyes clear again. He clutched her opal bracelet in his foreclaws.

"You good little thief," Phoebe said, taking the bracelet. When she did, a dull opal also tumbled from Mushroom's claw.

Blackerby grabbed the opal from the ground. "Is this Baron Ross's missing button?"

Phoebe helped Mushroom onto her shoulder. "Sudbury said something about the opals of dead men being a dragon poison, but Mushroom can't resist shiny things. He must have snatched it when we crashed."

"Good for Mushroom," Blackerby said. "But this puts a new light on the Luddite threat."

Westing looked perplexed for a moment, then his face went deathly pale.

"What is it?" Phoebe asked.

"We have a dragon-linked king who has been inexplicably ill for some time," Westing said in a low voice as if afraid the hedgerows were listening. "And the Prince Regent is dragon-linked as well."

Phoebe tightened her grip on Mushroom. "If the Luddites were able to hurt the king... Deborah was his key to getting close to the Prince Regent, too."

"Just so," Blackerby said. "I believe it is time for me to meet your Miss Sloan."

Chapter Twenty-Nine

THEY WAITED for Deborah at the Jaspers' townhouse in Grosvenor Street. Phoebe sat on the drawing-room sofa next to Westing close enough that their knees touched, which distracted her from the strain that hung over the room. Blackerby tapped his fingers on the arm of his chair, staring into the distance, while the Jaspers stood, both looking pale and dazed. Max had gone to visit a friend after delivering Deborah, ignorant of his sister's peril, so Farris fetched the girl.

The sound of footsteps reached them, and the first footman straightened. He wore a swollen lip and an enormous goose egg on his forehead, its brilliant red and purple matching the circles under his eyes—testaments to his noble efforts against Sudbury's invasion of the house. Lord Jasper had ordered him to take time off, but the footman insisted he had earned the right to continue his duties.

Deborah poked her head into the room. Wisps of blonde hair framed her pale face and wide, blue eyes. She cradled Rahab in her arms, and the pale-yellow dragon hissed at Westing and Blackerby's dragons, who lounged near the hearth.

Blackerby motioned for Deborah to sit. She looked at Phoebe, her eyes wide.

"You can trust them," Phoebe said. "I told them what I know or guess, but I think you had better let them know the whole of it."

"Miss... Sloan?" Blackerby asked.

She swallowed and shook her head. "It's Deborah Shaw, sir. I apologize for deceiving you, Miss Hart."

"Well, I knew Sloan wasn't your real name," Phoebe said.

Deborah looked surprised for a moment, then her eyes filled with tears. "You have been so good to me, and I have repaid you by letting you be kidnapped and—"

Blackerby held up a hand. "You may repent at leisure later, Miss Shaw. For now, we need to know whatever you can tell us about your uncle. Then, I promise we will do everything we can to protect you from him."

"That may not be enough," Deborah said, but she narrated for them her upbringing with Silas Shaw—Sudbury's real name —going into more detail about his experiments with Rahab, his leadership of the Luddites, and his plans for the Queen's Drawing-room. "So, I tried to hide from him and from Rahab."

Lord Jasper mumbled, "All under my own roof, and I was blind to it. My poor, brave Seraphina, left to face it alone."

Seraphina gave him a beatific smile, but Blackerby rolled his eyes and turned his attention back to Deborah.

"Your dragon is remarkable. The creature was relentless in its search for you. I believe it even managed to communicate with the White Dragon—either seeking its help or perhaps warning it of Sudbury—or Shaw's—threat."

Deborah looked at Rahab with appreciation, then her expression fell. "My uncle won't stop."

"Undoubtedly," Blackerby said. "Did Shaw ever speak of poisoning the king's dragon?"

Deborah's mouth opened, but she quickly shut it, looking

thoughtful. "Not to me, but it sounds like something he would do. He poisoned Rahab many times to see how it affected us."

For once, Deborah was subdued. Phoebe's heart ached for the girl.

"Do you know what he used?" Blackerby asked, his voice gentle.

"I'm sorry, I wish I did. If only I could help more after all the trouble I've caused." Some of the familiar Deborah was back.

"You have provided us with a useful weapon against him," Blackerby said. "Information. And we will put it to work immediately. I will increase the watch over all the food and drink brought to any of the royal family—and to their dragons— and we have the opal he wished to use. We'll deliver Shaw's description to every Bow Street Runner, constable, and justice of the peace in His Majesty's kingdom."

"He's good at disguises," Deborah said.

"You will help me know how to recognize him."

As Blackerby delved into deeper conversation with Deborah, Phoebe drew Westing into the antechamber. Dragon and Mushroom bounded ahead of them and curled up together on the sofa, a swirl of blue and green.

"Can Blackerby promise to keep Deborah safe?" Phoebe asked. "Sudbury... Shaw, I mean, seems desperately determined."

"I'm reasonably confident we can manage it."

"You and Lord Blackerby?"

"Blackerby, and you and I, darling." He took her hand and drew her closer. "Though I'm sure Joshua will be happy to help as well. And your brother."

"Hmm," Phoebe said, distracted by his thumb stroking the back of her hand. "You may be right, my lord."

"Much too formal, my heart. I won't ask you to call me Livermore, because it's a blasted awful name my father saddled me with, but it could at least be West. Something a little more endearing."

"Yes... West." She flushed with happiness. "But, how will we protect her?"

"Oh, I'll leave the ideas up to you. You have so many of them."

"Are you teasing me?"

He raised an eyebrow. "Would you like me to?"

She grinned, and he pulled her in for a kiss. And then another.

They were interrupted when Max stormed in through the drawing-room. "Hope you're happy! Miss Sloan is crying, telling me she ain't Miss Sloan anymore, and I can't make heads nor tails of—" He gave a startled yelp. "Cad! Unhand my sister!"

Phoebe's face heated. Westing broke away, laughing.

"It's very well for you to laugh," Max said. "Phoebe may be innocent, but I know your reputation, *rake*, and I won't have you toying with her." He took off a leather glove and tossed it at Westing's feet. "I'll see you at dawn for this!"

Westing stared down at the glove, his cheek twitching with an effort not to laugh. "Oh, it need not come to that. Since you have caught me, I suppose I must marry your sister. Will making her a viscountess satisfy the insult I have done to her?"

"Phoebe is worth more than any title you could—" Max glanced at his sister and stopped.

Phoebe, who had been biting her lip to keep from chuckling, met her brother's eye and burst into laughter.

Max's face softened. "Phoebs, were you *planning* on marrying him? And after the way you yelled at each other?"

She grabbed her brother's glove and handed it back to him. "I have quite a story to tell you, but yes, I am. Do you object, Max?"

"Well, dash it! I suppose I don't. But you could have at least warned me." Max turned to Westing. "You'd best take good care of her, sir."

"You have my word on that," Westing said, slipping an arm around Phoebe's shoulder.

"I think," Phoebe said to Max, "that my visit to London was a triumph after all."

"Why, you're a little minx!" Westing grinned and pulled her closer.

Phoebe laughed and leaned into his arms. Exactly where she belonged.

The Dragons of Mayfair continues in An Elusive Dragon.

Also by E.B. Wheeler

British Fiction:

The Haunting of Springett Hall

Born to Treason

The Royalist's Daughter

Wishwood (Westwood Gothic)

Moon Hollow (Westwood Gothic)

Utah Fiction:

No Peace with the Dawn (with Jeffery Bateman)

Bootleggers and Basil (in *The Pathways to the Heart*)

Letters from the Homefront

The Bone Map

Blood in a Dry Town (Tenny Mateo Mystery)

Balm of the Heart (in *In the Valley*)

Acknowledgments

Writing a book is never a solo process. I'm indebted to the readers and critique partners who provided support and feedback during the creation of this book, especially Dan, Karen, Lauren, and Melanie, and members of the Cache Valley Chapter of the League of Utah Writers, UPSSEFW, and the Clandestine Writers. And special thanks, as always, to my wonderful family for their ongoing support.

About the Author

E.B. Wheeler attended BYU, majoring in history with an English minor, and earned graduate degrees in history and landscape architecture from Utah State University. She's the award-winning author of *The Haunting of Springett Hall,* Whitney Award finalist *Born to Treason, Wishwood,* and *Moon Hollow,* as well as several short stories, magazine articles, and scripts for educational software programs. She was named the 2016 Writer of the Year by the League of Utah Writers. In addition to writing, she sometimes consults about historic preservation and teaches history at USU.

Find more about her books at ebwheeler.com

Made in United States
North Haven, CT
30 March 2023

34800411R00124